"Don't you believe in marriage at all?"

Suzanne continued, "You intend to give it a miss just because your father made a mistake?"

"I never said I intended to give marriage a miss," Dane corrected her. "I merely don't intend to rush into it because I happen to find a woman desirable."

"And when *do* you propose to rush into it?"

"When someone suitable comes along."

"Someone suitable," Suzanne thought aloud. She knew what that meant. Someone elegant, good-looking, with the right background. Someone who stood at the opposite end of the spectrum to her!

CATHY WILLIAMS is Trinidadian and was brought up on the twin islands of Trinidad and Tobago. She was awarded a scholarship to study in Britain, and went to Exeter University in 1975 to continue her studies into the great loves of her life: languages and literature. It was there that Cathy met her husband, Richard. Since they married, Cathy has lived in England—originally in the Thames Valley but now in the Midlands. Cathy and Richard have three small daughters.

Cathy Williams writes lively, sexy romances with heroes to die for! Look out for her next book in our EXPECTING miniseries, coming soon!

Books by Cathy Williams

CATHY WILLIAMS

A Suitable Mistress

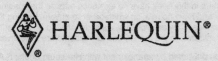

HARLEQUIN®

TORONTO • NEW YORK • LONDON
AMSTERDAM • PARIS • SYDNEY • HAMBURG
STOCKHOLM • ATHENS • TOKYO • MILAN • MADRID
PRAGUE • WARSAW • BUDAPEST • AUCKLAND

ISBN 0-373-12006-0

A SUITABLE MISTRESS

First North American Publication 1999.

CHAPTER ONE

ANOTHER bad day. Another bad week. Suzanne sat down on the edge of the bed and wondered when things were ever going to get better. She surely must have hit rock bottom now. Surely the law of averages said that things had to improve. No one could keep going downhill for ever.

At some point in time, one would crash-land somewhere at the bottom of the deep, dark well, and wouldn't be able to go any further. Which, she thought tiredly, still left unanswered the question of how exactly you got out of the well, but presumably you would be so relieved not to be still falling that you wouldn't give that too much hard thought.

Right now, though, she didn't feel relieved. She felt trapped and hopeless, just as she had felt for the past six months.

She raised her head slightly and caught a glimpse of herself in the mirror opposite and looked away hurriedly.

She hated having to face what her head repeatedly told her. That she had let herself go. She hadn't meant to; it seemed to be something that had happened when she hadn't been looking, almost when she had had her back turned. She had put on weight, her long hair was neat enough but uninspiring and she knew that she appeared tired, even when she was forcing herself to put recent events behind her and show a smiling face to the world.

She reached inside her handbag, extracted a bar of

chocolate, and, steeling herself not to think back, painstakingly removed the wrapper and bit into it, hardly tasting the sweetness, simply content that the sheer movement of eating helped to distract her from the tears which were lurking so close to the surface.

I've thrown in my accountancy course, she thought, rewrapping the uneaten bit of chocolate left with the same painstaking motions. I've come here to London in search of streets paved with gold, only to find that there's no such thing, and to top it all I've now just lost my job. But there must be a bright side somewhere to this. She frowned and scoured her mind for the odd silver lining or two, and then told herself that she had hated that wretched job anyway.

She had just been a dogsbody, running around and doing all those untidy, boring chores which no one else wanted to do. The downside was that, however hateful it had been, it had at least been a source of income and now, without it, she gloomily contemplated a scenario of unpaid bills, bailiffs, screaming landladies and probably a park bench somewhere with only her pillow and a blanket for company.

It was, she admitted to herself, a fairly ludicrous scenario, since she would not allow herself to be without work, but she dwelled on it anyway, listlessly aware that she should really get out of the bedsit and do something instead of sitting like a block of lead on her bed and letting inertia get the better of her. A block, she thought with a flash of that irony which had recently deserted her, of overweight lead.

She stood up and walked across to the dreaded mirror and made herself look at the reflection staring out at her. There had been a time once, in a past which she couldn't bear thinking about, when she had been attractive. Long, wavy dark hair, bright blue eyes, a slim, tall figure. Look at you now, she said to herself critically. Your hair desperately needs a trim, your eyes lack sparkle and you're hardly going to win Miss Slender of the Year, are you?

She was still examining herself and telling herself that she really would go to the hairdressers, that she really would stop eating junk food which was doing absolutely nothing for her, when she heard someone knocking on the door. Very loud knocking. Knocking which instantly brought to mind screaming landladies. Or rather, just the one screaming landlady who seemed to have mastered the trick of avoiding complaints, while still vociferously demanding rent at least a week before it fell due.

You are not going to cower, she told herself sternly. You live in a bedsit which is in a fairly appalling condition, with a fridge that either freezes everything solid or else insists on defrosting at inconvenient times, and besides, you're bigger than she is.

She strode purposefully towards the door, pulled it open, mentally steeled herself to say something about the fridge, not to mention the curtains which looked as though they were leftovers from the Stone Age, and stepped back in shock at the man standing outside the room.

She felt her face go scarlet and she knew that she was gaping, but for the life of her she couldn't think of a thing to say.

Dane Sutherland was the very last person she had expected to see standing outside her door and she was conscious of a rush of awareness at the mere sight of him. Tall, dark and shamelessly good-looking, he was the last person she wanted to see.

'What are you doing here?' she asked the figure lounging indolently against the doorframe and making the dingy hallway look even dingier than it was.

'I've had a hard time finding you.'

Still the same old voice that she remembered from years back. Deep, velvety, with a trace of dry mockery

lurking there somewhere. He could charm the birds off
the trees with that voice of his—a voice that held just
enough lazy sensuality, a promise of things unspoken.
She had watched from the sidelines just how many birds
he had charmed off the trees as he had moved through
adolescence into maturity. How utterly and childishly
aware she had been of him.

It was difficult to know when exactly he had moved
from the uncomplicated position of being her brother's
friend into the vastly more complicated one of being a
deeply attractive person of the opposite sex.

She could remember when she was fourteen, looking
at him surreptitiously from under her lashes, aware of
him in a way that she had not been before: aware of him
as a man, a first-year university graduate no less, already
with the sort of cool, ironic self-assurance which gave
him a maturity that her brother had lacked.

'I suppose I had better ask you in,' she said ungraciously, averting her eyes and walking back into the
room, leaving him to shut the door. 'I'm afraid I only
have tea,' she said, disliking his presence in her flat,
disliking everything about him, and determined to be as
churlish and unwelcoming as she felt she could reasonably get away with.

'Tea would be fine.' He followed her into the kitchen,
which was barely big enough for one person and with
him standing there felt chokingly claustrophobic.

She made them both mugs of tea, politely waited until
he went back into the small sitting room, and then
flopped into the chair furthest away from him.

'I was very sorry to hear about your father's death,'
he murmured, watching her intently with those grey,
steely eyes, and she could feel the tears gathering momentum at the back of her throat. Again. Every time, in
fact, she thought about her father.

'I would have liked to have come to the funeral,' he

continued, looking at her over the rim of his cup, 'but I was in New York at the time, and I just couldn't make it.'

Suzanne shrugged. 'I wouldn't have expected you to put yourself out,' she said coldly. 'After all, he was just your family's chauffeur, for heaven's sake.' Just the chauffeur who had worked for them nearly all his life; just the chauffeur who had lived in their cottage and pottered around in their garden; just the chauffeur who had collapsed and died in the line of duty.

'Why on earth do you continue working for her?' she had once asked her father.

'Old Mr Sutherland would have wanted it,' he had told her, which had made absolutely no sense to her at all. Old Mr Sutherland, she had wanted to point out, was dead, and had been for some time, and now his wife, or rather his second wife, was in charge, and she was an awful woman.

But she had not said anything because they had covered that ground before, and she had known what his answer would be: he was too old now to change, and besides, he liked the house, he liked the grounds, he liked the calm and peace of the countryside. So he had continued to work there, doing whatever the grand lady of the house wanted, which mostly had nothing to do with driving and much more to do with tending the lawns and taking the wretched poodles for walks and repairing whatever needed repair in the great mansion.

And all for what? Martha Sutherland hadn't even attended the funeral. She had been busy getting ready for a cruise and had made unalterable plans. So a wreath had been sent in her place. A huge, gaudy one. And Dane, who had known him virtually since birth, had been busy as well. Because, after all, he was just their chauffeur, wasn't he?

Her mind jumped back to that overheard conversation, and she closed the door on it.

She gave Dane a tinny, frozen smile and waited for him to ask her what she meant, but he ignored the pointed sarcasm behind her remark, although his eyes narrowed on her in a way that made her feel just a little bit ashamed that she had said what she had.

'I thought you were working with that firm of accountants in the town,' he said, and she shrugged and looked away.

'I packed it in when Dad died.' She had been so utterly miserable, and studying to qualify as an accountant—something of which her father had been so proud—had suddenly seemed trivial and meaningless. She had never been entirely sure that that was what she had wanted to do, and without her father's encouragement she had been gripped by the thought that it was a career which had found her rather than the other way around. She had always been clever with figures and she had settled into accountancy the way that some people settle into marriage—because it was convenient.

'Why?'

'Because I wanted to leave the area. Is that a good enough explanation for you? Or would you like to pursue it further?' She had had a plan, she thought defensively. Where had it gone? How could it have evaporated so quickly, like mist? How could she have ended up like a lost soul wandering in a fog, when she had started out with such determination?

'And you think that he would have been happy to see you living like this?' He looked around him at the scrappy room, with its sad, faded rug in front of the fireplace and skirting-boards which were in desperate need of a lick of paint. The bare essentials were so in need of repair that they sabotaged her every effort to make the bedsit into something warm and comfortable. The most she could achieve was neatness.

'What have you come here for?' she asked abruptly.

'I wanted to offer my condolences personally to you, and I admit I was worried when they told me that you had walked out of the company.'

'So you decided to fit me into your schedule. Big of you,' she said acidly. Shame, she thought, that he had never been big enough to see that her father got a fair deal working for his stepmother. Shame that he hadn't been big enough to listen to her father when he'd started getting tired for no reason. Shame that he hadn't been big enough to let him retire in that cottage, instead of allowing his stepmother to imply that once the old man could no longer function he would have to move out and make way for someone who could.

The threat of having nowhere to live had been enough to keep her father on his toes, when in fact he should have been resting far more than he had been.

She swallowed down the great lump of resentment in her and stared down into the cup of lukewarm tea. The milk was gathering itself into a fine brown film. She inspected the film with minute concentration.

'Shall I continue to ignore your acid little rejoinders, Suzie, or would you be happier if I gave in and indulged your desire to have a blazing row over nothing?'

'Nothing!' Her head shot up at that one and she looked at him with savage dislike. 'How dare you sit here and say that? I've lost the only person in my life who has ever meant anything to me and you call that nothing? That stepmother of yours treated him like a workhorse and you call that nothing? He was old and frail and he should have had the dignity of being able to enjoy the rest of his days in that cottage of yours, without thinking that if he stopped lugging ladders and walking poodles he would no longer have a roof over his head.'

He stood up and walked across to the window and stared out, and although she couldn't see the set of his face she could tell by the rigidity of his shoulders that he was angry.

'I don't like what you're implying here,' he said with disarming softness, turning round to face her. The light behind him threw his face into shadows and lent it an air of dark menace.

'Then you're free to leave.' She nodded in the direction of the door and she was perversely pleased when he remained where he was, because, for the first time in the six months since her father had died, she was shouting, and glad to be shouting.

'He loved your father,' she threw at him. 'Why do you think he continued working there, even when your father remarried three years ago? Why do you think he stayed there after your father died?'

'I have been out of the country for nearly three years,' Dane said in a controlled voice that didn't quite manage to hide the undercurrent of anger and impatience at her accusations. 'I had it on my stepmother's word that everything at the house was fine.'

'And that was the extent of your interest in the place?' she asked bitterly. 'And how thrilled your dad would have been with that!'

He moved more quickly than she could have expected. One minute he was standing there at the window, and the next minute he was leaning over her, his hands resting on either side of the chair.

'Now you listen to me, my girl,' he said tersely. 'I haven't come here to have an argument with you. Nor have I come here to be attacked for things I knew nothing of.'

'In three years you never returned once to see for

yourself how everything was, to check and make sure
that people were happy!'

'I had my reasons,' he said grimly, still leaning over
her, so that she began to feel something else mingling
with her anger—something faint and disturbing which
made her even more angry because she didn't want to
feel it.

She had been through that childish, excited infatuation
with Dane Sutherland, and she had been disabused of it
in no uncertain terms. She had no intention of letting
dead embers re-ignite.

He might stand there and plead innocence to everything she said, but he must have known what was going
on at Chadwick House. He must have known about the
loyal help who had been sacked virtually the day after
his father had died. He must have known of the promises
made by his father to his workers, which had never been
kept.

Old Mr Sutherland had promised her father the cottage. A gentleman's agreement, because although her father had been his employee the two had been com-
rades—old friends who would sit and have a cup of tea
and lament the passing of time with the shared memories
of old men.

Dane must have known that his stepmother had put
paid to any such agreement not five months after her
husband had died. He must have known because Dane
Sutherland was an intelligent man, frighteningly intelligent, and, after all, the house was his. She couldn't believe, whatever he said, that he had cut himself off so
completely from his past.

'What the hell are you doing here, Suzie?' he asked,
straightening up and giving her time to compose her face
and get her nervous system back in order again.

'What do you mean?'

'I mean,' he said, sitting down on the sofa and

crossing his legs, one ankle over his knee, 'you're a highly intelligent girl. You could have gone to university, but you chose to stay close to your father and apprentice in a company instead. You were doing damned well at it. So why did you throw it all in and move to London?'

'You forget,' she replied coolly, 'that I no longer had a roof over my head. Your stepmother made it crystal-clear that she wanted the cottage back and the sooner I cleared out of it the better.'

'Dammit, Suzie, you should have written to me in New York.' He raked his fingers through his hair—a restless, impatient gesture that she could remember him making even as a teenager. Whenever he was angry over something. Her brother had tried to cultivate it, but somehow he had never managed to convey the same magnetic, effortless charm.

'Thank you,' she said politely, 'but I haven't resorted to asking for charity as yet. Besides, I couldn't honestly imagine a worse hell than living in the vicinity of your stepmother.'

She thought of Martha Sutherland with distaste. Brassy blonde and, at thirty-two, less than half the age of the man she had married. She was the sort of woman whose nails were always impeccably varnished in red, and who never set foot out of the house without being sure that everything about her co-ordinated.

'So you threw away your future and moved into a grimy bedsit in London instead.'

'You don't understand,' she snapped.

'I understand better than you think.'

'After seeing me for the first time in years and after only forty-five minutes. What a genius you must be at reading other people's characters.'

She hated this conversation and she wished that she could just take refuge in some of that uneaten chocolate lying in her bag. Then, for the first time since he had entered the room, she wondered what he must think, seeing her now. Seeing how much she had changed physically. She knew that he had never found her attractive; she just wasn't his type—too tall, too gauche, too dark-haired—but what must he think of her now? Overweight, hair unflatteringly pulled back, dressed in dark colours which she knew did nothing for her—somehow she had lost the will to dress with any attempt at style.

She shoved aside the temptation to reach for her bag and extract the chocolate and contented herself with glaring at him.

'What are you doing for money?' he asked, looking at her with lazy speculation.

'I have a job,' she said sullenly. 'I've been temping since I moved down here.' She linked her fingers on her lap and frowned. Now that she had begun thinking about the changes he must see in her—all for the worse—she found that she couldn't stop herself. She was acutely aware that her once flat stomach was not so flat as it had been, that her legs and thighs were filling out her trousers in a way that implied that if she continued snacking off bars of chocolate she would soon find herself moving up a size in clothes. Again.

'Doing what, exactly?'

'Doing whatever pays the rent. Exactly.'

'But nothing to do with accountancy.'

'I resent your criticisms,' she told him resentfully. 'You have no right to march in here and start telling me what I'm doing wrong with my life. Your zeal to do good would have been far more useful a year ago. In fact, it might have saved my father's life.'

A heavy silence greeted this, but he was saved from having to say anything because someone knocked at the or and she leapt to her feet, carefully keeping her eyes firmly averted from his face.

It never paid to antagonise Dane Sutherland too much. He was a controlled person but when he was angry he could be immensely frightening. Once, when Dane was fifteen, the school bully had made the mistake, never again repeated, of making some sly, sneering remark about old Mr Sutherland. Dane hadn't raised a finger. He hadn't had to. He had just gone very close to him and said something which, hovering on the sidelines with two of her friends, she had not heard, but which had been enough to scare Tim Chapman into complete silence.

Thinking about it, she realised that he hadn't bullied anyone again after that. In fact, when she'd last laid eyes on him he'd been a rather harassed father of four working at the garage outside town. Rumour had it that his wife took his money off him as soon as it landed in his hands and then doled it out to him as she saw fit.

She was almost relieved to see her landlady standing outside with her hands on her hips and a belligerent expression on her face. Almost, but not quite. The rent was, for once, late and money was, as always, thin on the ground.

'I've been trying to get hold of you for the past four days,' Mrs Gentry said, in that voice of hers which sent shivers of apprehension down her tenants' spines, even when they had done nothing wrong.

'I'm a bit behind this month with the rent, Mrs Gentry,' Suzanne said, taking the bull by the horns.

'You could say so.' She pursed her lips and said in a reedy voice, 'There's many who would jump at the chance of renting this bedsit, I don't have to tell you that. I warned you when I took you on that there was a lot of competition for this place; there's many who would stand for days queuing up outside to rent here. It's a prime area to be—'

'Oh, really.'

Suzanne had never seen anyone make the landlady's mouth fall open, but Dane did.

He stood next to her, with his hands in his pockets and a cold smile on his lips.

'And I,' he continued icily, 'have yet to meet anyone prepared to stomach the downright primitive conditions of this dump, which you have the nerve to glorify by calling a bedsit.' Mrs Gentry was staring at him, disconcerted and alarmed and shuffling from one foot to the other.

'There's many—' she began, with an attempt to recapture some of her authority, and he cut her off swiftly.

'Who are willing to put up with this ghastly hole simply because they have no choice. And there are some, of whom I am one, who would be more than willing to take you to court for renting out a place like this.'

'Of course I would be more than prepared to fix a few things, more than prepared, if the miss here had complained—'

'The fridge doesn't work, Mrs Gentry,' Suzanne interjected swiftly. 'I mentioned that to you four months ago and I've been mentioning it every time I've seen you since.'

'Of course,' Mrs Gentry blustered, 'I was about to say to you that I'll have that fridge taken away and replaced. I've been meaning to do it for some time, sir—' she reverted her attention to Dane, clearly at a disadvantage because he was so much taller than she was and she had to crane her neck upwards to look at him '—but I've been off my head with worry these last few months, what with the husband and his drinking problems.'

Husband? Drinking problems? This was the first that Suzanne had heard of any such thing. In fact, she was sure that Mrs Gentry lived on her own, probably having nagged her husband into the ground.

'I'll have the rent for you by the weekend,' Suzanne said, aware that she would have to cope with the redoubtable Mrs Gentry all on her own, once Dane had gone, and not willing to stir up too much bad feeling just in case she found herself without living quarters. The woman, worse luck, was right when she said that places were hard to get in London, and even this bedsit, appalling though it was, was better than some she had seen.

'It's already late,' Mrs Gentry pointed out, on safer ground now. 'I'll overlook that, though, if I can have it in my hands no later than Saturday midday.' She stepped back slightly and then said with a sly smile, 'However, I'm afraid that I'm going to have to raise the rent from next month. Inflation, you know.' She told Suzanne how much extra she would have to pay, and it wasn't until she had straddled off, in search of another victim, that Suzanne sat down on the sofa with a groan of despair.

'I shall never be able to afford it,' she said. 'Where am I going to get that money from?' Especially now that I no longer have a job, she added silently to herself.

'It's hardly a vast sum of money,' Dane pointed out reasonably, and she glared at him with loathing. Of course, she wanted to say, it wasn't a vast sum of money, but it was just enough to make her standard of living very uncomfortable indeed if she was forced to find it out of her now non-existent salary.

'Not to you,' she told him sourly. 'You already have vast sums of money, but I haven't and it's a great deal to me.'

'Why don't you ask for a pay rise?'

'A pay rise?' Her eyebrows flew up and she laughed drily. 'If you must know, that would be very difficult, since as of today I have joined the ranks of the unemployed.' She stood up and fetched both empty mugs and walked towards the kitchen, throwing over her shoulder. 'But that's no problem. I shall simply have to dig into my minuscule savings account and make do.'

It wasn't something that she wanted. She wasn't holding onto her savings for anything in particular, but she felt more cushioned knowing that the money was there, even if it wasn't a great deal. She regarded it as money which she might need for a rainy day. It was a blow to think that the rainy day would turn out to be a bedsit in London and Mrs Gentry's grasping hands. But what choice did she have?

'How did you manage to lose your job?' he asked, when she returned to the little sitting room.

'Isn't it about time that you left? Consider your condolences personally delivered.'

She ignored the self-righteous little voice in her head and dug inside her handbag for the remainder of the chocolate, which she ate slowly, not caring what he thought of her eating habits. Or her weight problem, for that matter.

'Answer my question.'

'Oh, all right!' she snapped, looking at him. How easy everything was for him. Born into wealth, blessed with looks and intelligence. She disliked him sitting there trying to drag conversation out of her when she would much rather have preferred solitude, a little time to consider her position—a little time, the self-righteous voice told her, to feel sorry for herself all over again.

'I had an argument with my supervisor,' she admitted. 'And I won't bother to pretend that it wasn't my fault. I didn't like the way that he was doing things. There were no controls and he preferred going down to the pub to trying to get things into order. I told him so and he sacked me on the spot. I had to leave as I was only a temp.'

A ghost of a smile flitted across her face as she remembered the encounter. Mike Slattery was an odious little man with a sharp, ratlike face and a tendency to issue orders. It had been wonderful to give him the benefit of her opinions, even if it had cost her her job.

'You were always outspoken,' Dane drawled, surveying her from under thick, dark lashes. 'Always ready to rush in where angels feared to tread. Which,' he continued, 'doesn't solve the problem of what you're going to do now.'

Suzanne shrugged and contemplated the empty chocolate wrapper ruefully.

'I'll manage.'

'And continue to live here?'

She followed his scathing glance round the room and said angrily, 'You'd be surprised what a palace this is in comparison to some places that I've seen! At least the roof is one piece and there's a carpet of sorts on the floor.' A far cry from her father's cottage. Was Dane thinking that too?

She looked down, blinking rapidly. Her father had been so upset when Martha Sutherland had announced that the cottage would revert to the house in due course. A gorgeous summer retreat for weekend guests, she had told him, patting her blonde hair and rearranging the decor in her mind's eye.

Where had Dane been when her father had needed him? Or maybe he had known of his stepmother's intentions all along, and had silently gone along with them, letting her do the dirty work while he built empires in America.

'You can't continue to wallow in grief for the rest of your life,' he said, looking at her, unperturbed by the outrage on her face which his remark engendered.

'How dare you? I am not wallowing in grief!'

'I understand,' he continued calmly, 'how upset you

must have been by your father's death, but allowing your life to crumble is not going to bring him back.'

Suzanne's mouth thinned and she wanted to hit him. No one had told her anything like that. At the funeral they had all been so kind and understanding. Even Mr Barnes had sympathised when she'd told him that she was going to leave the company and move down to London.

Her friends had understood as well. She frowned. She hadn't contacted any of them, she realised, since she had left Warwickshire—at first because she literally hadn't been able to bring herself to talk to anyone, and then later because time had elapsed and she had just not got around to it. Most of them had grown up with her. They had all been there at the funeral. She would get in touch with them, she decided, soon.

'Life goes on, Suzie,' he said, refusing to release the topic even though her stormy blue eyes were telling him to. 'You can't continue holding onto your anger and grief, while life slides past.'

'Stop preaching to me!' She got up and restlessly walked to the bay window in the sitting room and stared outside for a while. 'I didn't ask you to come here,' she told him, turning around and half sitting on the window-ledge, with her arms folded and her face mutinous. 'I'm getting on with my life and everything is just fine!'

'You are not getting on with your life,' Dane said, with the same infuriating calm, as if he were talking to a wilful child in need of appeasement. 'You gave up your course, you now no longer have a job down here...' His grey eyes raked over her and she flushed, knowing what he was going to say next and resenting it already. 'And I needn't tell you the obvious: you've looked better.'

That brought tears of hurt anger to her eyes, even though she could hardly disagree with what he said.

He paused, thoughtfully, head cocked to one side as though trying out an idea in his head and wondering whether it would fit. 'You are going to leave this place,' he said decisively. 'You are going to come back to my apartment in London, where I am now living, until you find somewhere more salubrious to live. You are going to work for one of my London subsidiaries and you are not going to chuck it in for any reason whatsoever.'

Suzanne stared at him in complete silence and then said, in as civilised a tone as she could muster, 'You must be mad.'

'You might just as well pack now and leave with me. It shouldn't take long. I don't see too many personal possessions strewn around.'

'I am not coming anywhere with you!' she said in a high, unsteady voice. 'I'm not going to accept charity from you.' The way my poor father did, her tone implied. And just look at what he got for it, she thought. He died an unhappy man, thanks to your wretched stepmother. Your family was responsible, like it or not.

'You are going to do just exactly as I tell you,' he said, standing up.

'Why? Why should I?'

'Because I say so.'

'And your word is gospel?' She laughed with sarcasm, and he reached out and gripped her arm.

'I know you want to blame someone for your father's death,' he ground out, 'and I know that you have decided that I fit the bill. Fine. It's a misconception which you will grow out of with time. But I have no intention of letting you stay here a minute longer and that's that. So start packing your bags. You're coming with me.'

'I don't intend to be bullied by you!'

'Someone has to bully you into doing something,' he said impatiently. 'If your brother was here instead of in Australia the task would fall to him.'

'Task? Task? So I'm a responsibility now, am I? Poor little Suzanne Stanton who has no control over her life.'

'That's right.'

She glared at him and had the sinking feeling that arguing would be like trying to make a dent with a wooden spoon in the Rock of Gibraltar. He was immovable. He had waltzed in here, decided that she was unfit to take control of herself and had immediately concluded, probably because he felt guilty, that the onerous task fell to him.

'I don't need your pity,' she said bitingly, 'or anyone else's for that matter.'

'You're a child, Suzie,' he told her by way of response. 'You don't know what you need. You should thank God that I have returned to take you in hand.'

CHAPTER TWO

A BULLY. That, she decided, was what Dane was. An
overgrown bully. Suzanne sat next to him in the car,
simmering with resentment, and he calmly ignored it all
and made polite conversation, asking her questions, pris-
ing answers reluctantly out of her.

The very worst thing was that she knew that she was
behaving like a child. His proposition might have gone
against everything ingrained in her, everything that told
her that he was part of the family that had mistreated
her father, but his offer was better than anything that she
could come up with herself: a roof over her head and a
job.

And the memory of Mrs Gentry's face when she'd
told her that she could keep her awful little bedsit af-
forded her quite a bit of silent amusement. She glanced
across at him in the dark car and felt a shiver of alarmed
apprehension. He was, to himself at any rate, doing her
a favour and there was nothing, she told herself, that she
should be alarmed about, but she had the uneasy feeling
of being a fish in a net—a very large net at this point in
time, with lots of room for manoeuvre, but a net nev-
ertheless.

He looked across at her and she dropped her eyes
quickly.

'How long did Tom stay after your father's funeral?'
he asked casually. He had, she noticed, no qualms at all
about referring to her father's death. Most people stu-

diously avoided mentioning it, as though it were a strangely taboo subject.

'Only a fortnight,' she replied, looking out of the window at London passing slowly by her—crowded streets, brightly lit shops, a sense of hurry everywhere. 'Marian couldn't come over. She's eight months pregnant and six months ago they told her that she couldn't travel. He wanted to get back to her as soon as he could.'

She thought regretfully of her brother's hurried stay in England. It would have been comforting to have him around for a bit longer, although things between them had changed slightly anyway. He was married now and had been for three years.

He had sent their father a ticket to Australia so that he could go to the wedding. She remembered with deep fondness the state of great excitement that had preceded the departure. Anyone would have thought that he had been picked to fly to the moon.

But marriage had taken Tom away a bit from her. They still chatted easily, and wrote to each other often, but his attentions no longer focused on his little sister as indulgently as they had. He had a wife now—a wife whom she had never met although the pictures of her promised someone very friendly—and a baby on the way.

'He asked me to go back with him,' she said suddenly, leaning a bit against the door so that she could look at Dane's averted profile.

'Why didn't you?'

'It seemed like the end of the world and beyond.' At the time she had felt that to go that far away would be somehow tantamount to desertion. 'Besides,' she added, terminating the conversation because she could see it leading to another sermon on how far she had let herself go, simply because, after all these months, she still

couldn't muster up the enthusiasm to do anything, however hard she tried, 'I hate huge spiders.'

'I suspect there's probably more to Australia than
huge spiders,' he said drily, half smiling, and she had
that unpleasant, falling feeling which she could remember as a teenager, when he had smiled at her in a way
that made her feel as though he had access to all her
deepest thoughts.

'Why did you decide to go to America?' she asked,
changing the subject, and his face hardened.

'I had my reasons,' he said in his usual, controlled
voice, but there was an edge of granite there that hadn't
been there before.

'What reasons?' she asked with interest, and he
frowned and glanced across at her.

'I see that tact still isn't one of your strong points,'
he said with lazy amusement.

'Why should you feel free to ask questions about my
life and I can't do the same about yours?'

'Because you're a child and children shouldn't ask too
many questions.' He laughed but she didn't laugh with
him.

'What you're saying is that, since I should be indebted
to you, I should just bow my head in silence and accept
what the master tells me without asking anything in return?'

'That's rubbish,' he told her calmly. 'But, if you really
want to know, I went away to make my fortune.'

'I thought that your father left you everything?' He
had drawn the lines and she knew that she was over-
stepping them but he was right, tact never had been one
of her strong points, and besides, she had no intention
of allowing him to think that she had to be subservient
simply because her father had worked for his.

She was grudgingly aware that she was being slightly
unfair in this generalisation, but every time she thought

of him she thought of his stepmother and the blood rushed to her head with angry force.

'He left me the estate and a fair-sized inheritance, but control of the company went to Martha.'

'I'm surprised that she didn't ask you to take over,' Suzanne said. He had run it virtually single-handed for the four years before his father died.

'Oh, there were a lot of things that Martha wanted,' he said coolly, and this time the warning in his voice left her in no doubt that he did not intend to develop the conversation further. 'But we don't always get what we want in life, do we? I decided to make my own fortune in America.'

'And you did.'

'And,' he said, turning to her briefly, 'I did.'

They had been driving through a very exclusive part of London for the past few minutes. The sort of place that made a very convincing show of being in the country somewhere. Lots of trees and houses hidden from public sight by walls and hedges and long, swirling drives.

The car turned into one of the long, swirling drives and her eyes widened as she took in the proportions of the house. It was huge. A great Victorian building that had been converted into apartments.

No wonder the pitiful increase in rent with which Mrs Gentry had threatened her had seemed a paltry affair to him.

There was a security guard on the ground floor, sitting at a desk and surrounded by various strategically placed plants and a few pieces of discreet furniture here and there. It looked like someone's lounge.

'Are you allowed to have guests staying with you?' she asked in a whisper as they took the lift up to his floor, and he looked at her with a mixture of amusement and irony.

'This entire block of apartments belongs to me,' he said. 'An investment purchase made two weeks after I left the country.'

'You knew you would come back?'

'Oh, yes,' he said with a smile that held no warmth, 'I knew that I would come back. The only question was when.'

She looked at him, vaguely feeling that there was something here, something not being said, that carried a wealth of hidden meaning, but she couldn't put her finger on it and he was not about to elucidate. He would never reveal anything unless he wanted to. It was what, she suspected, made him so formidable.

She followed him out of the lift, along the thick white carpet, and it transpired that the entire floor of the building comprised his apartment.

Four bedrooms, two bathrooms, an office, a lounge, a kitchen, all beautifully furnished, ready and waiting, she thought, for Dane Sutherland when he decided that the time was right to return.

Suzanne dropped her little battered case in the lounge and looked around her with amazement.

'No wonder you thought that the bedsit was dingy,' she said, turning to face him.

'The bedsit *was* dingy,' he drawled. He had removed his jacket and rolled up the sleeves of his white shirt to the elbows so that his powerful forearms were exposed, and she ignored the sudden quickening of her pulses.

'Well, it's certainly an eye-opener to see how the other half lives,' she said honestly, and he frowned with impatience.

'Let's get one thing straight,' he said, not moving from where he was standing, tall, muscled and disturbing at the other end of the room. 'You're going to be living here. Your rooms will be quite separate from mine, and I shall be out of the apartment most of the time so we probably will only see one another in passing, but when we do cross paths I do not expect to be bombarded with a litany of badly veiled insults. Do you understand?'

'There's no need to talk to me as though I was a child,' Suzanne said, mouth turned down.

'Then you'll have to get out of the habit of acting like one.' He walked towards her, picked up her three suitcases and said, over his shoulder, 'I'll show you to your room.'

He'd been right about her being separate from him. Her room, which also included a bathroom and another small room off it which had been converted into a sitting room with a television, was at the opposite end of the block.

She looked around her and said, with her back to him, fingering the wonderful patchwork bedspread, which looked as though it had leapt straight out of the pages of an interior decoration magazine, 'How much rent would you like me to pay?'

'Don't be ridiculous.' There was impatience in his voice and she spun round.

'I have to pay you something,' she answered stubbornly. 'I can't live here for nothing.'

'I don't want your money,' he grated. 'I've known you since you were in nappies. Do you think I expect you to pay me for the privilege of being provided with a roof over your head?'

'No more charity from your family,' she muttered, meeting his hard grey eyes levelly.

I've learnt a lesson from my father, she thought. What's given with one hand is taken with the other.

'There's no point in letting pride get in the way of judgement, Suzie,' he said, not angrily but as though he was explaining something to a child.

'Without pride, we are nothing.'

'And from what book did you pick up that little gem?'

She flushed angrily, thinking that she had read it somewhere and it had seemed like a damned good piece of wisdom at the time.

'I'll pay you what I paid Mrs Gentry,' she told him. 'I know it's not a quarter of what it's worth, but it's all I can afford. Don't think that you can ease your conscience over my father's treatment by letting me live here free of charge.'

'Oh, for God's sake! Buy something for the place once a month. Would that satisfy your pride?'

She gave it some thought and nodded. 'All right,' she conceded, lifting her chin, and he ran his fingers through his hair.

'Now would you like something to eat? Or would the food stick in your throat?'

Was he laughing at her? There was no smile on his face, but it was difficult to tell with him.

'Would you like me to cook?' she offered, and he raised his eyebrows sceptically.

'Can you cook? I remember when you were thirteen you cooked something for Tom and me and it was a bit of a struggle to get through the meal.'

'Very funny.' Why did he still treat her as though she was a child? she wondered crossly. Rescuing her from her unpleasant bedsit, talking to her as though her wits were very slightly scrambled.

'What was it you cooked?' He was still amused at the memory, and she followed him into the kitchen, watching the lean build of his body, the way he moved with panther-like grace, every movement silent and economical.

'Roast chicken,' she replied, determined not to act the sullen child any more than she could help. 'It burnt.' Everything had burnt. She had turned the oven too high. The only salvageable item had been the gravy. She could remember how mortified she had been, infatuated with this dark, devastatingly handsome university graduate, clumsy and thirteen, with long, gangly limbs and long, unruly hair which she had tied up because she had thought that it made her look older.

'Your father was a superb cook,' he said, extracting various things from the fridge after he had made her sit down. 'When you were very young, he used to try out dishes on your brother and me. At the time we thought most of them a bit odd, but they tasted excellent.'

He wasn't looking at her. He was busy doing something that involved chopping and opening of cans, but he expected a reply. She sensed rather than knew that.

'Yes, he was a wonderful cook,' she agreed, feeling that lump in her throat again. She fished inside her handbag and took out a block of chocolate, doing it surreptitiously. She wasn't accustomed to talking about her father. She had bottled up her emotions inside her ever since his death and it was painful to voice her memories, even when the questions asked were so detached.

She lapsed into her memories and licked her fingers absent-mindedly after she had finished eating the chocolate. She was only aware that Dane was looking at her when she glanced up, her eyes dry, and she said defensively, 'I'm going to go on a diet.'

He didn't say anything, which annoyed her more than if he had. He just nodded to two of the cupboards, asked her to set the table, and then returned to what he was doing.

Suzanne got up, feeling instantly lumpy after that forbidden piece of chocolate, and began putting plates and cutlery down.

'I know that I've put on a bit of weight,' she said into what she thought was a critical silence. 'It's simply that I've got into the habit of snacking recently.' Well, for months, she said to herself. Eating all the wrong things and justifying it by telling herself that she would start a

sensible diet tomorrow. She tried to neaten her hair with
one hand and decided that it was an impossible task. Her
hair never did what it was told.

'There's no need to justify yourself,' he said, bringing
food to the table. He deposited two saucepans, one of
which contained spaghetti and the other a red sauce
smelling of garlic. He had opened a bottle of wine and
he poured them both a glass, then sat down so that he
was directly facing her.

'I wasn't justifying myself,' Suzanne began, confused.
'I was simply explaining...' Her voice trailed off and
she helped herself to some of the pasta and the sauce. 'I
happen to like the way I look,' she continued.

Why did he insist on making her feel so defensive and
indignant? she wondered. Why couldn't he have left her
to muddle along to her own devices? She didn't need
his help to pull herself together. She would have done
it quite completely on her own. After a while. Why did
he have to come along and feel sorry for her? She didn't
want to be an object of pity. He didn't owe her anything
and she wished that he had just left her alone. Just because he had known her since she'd been in nappies
didn't mean that he now owed her something.

'You've changed too, you know,' she said accusingly,
after a while.

And she was taken aback when he leaned back in the
chair and said with an amused, lazy smile, 'Have I? Tell
me how.'

Suzanne stared at him with the drowning feeling of
having got into something that was beyond her depth.

She tried not to look addled but the only thing her
mind would tell her was that, if anything, he had become
even more devastatingly handsome than she remembered. His dark good looks had hardened, taken on the
indefinable edge of power and control.

'You look older,' she said lamely.

'I am older.' He waited, amused.

'Of course, you're still—still…an attractive man…' She gave her full attention to a mouthful of spaghetti, thinking what an undignified meal it was, especially when only one of you was doing the eating.

He threw back his head and laughed. 'Dear me, how embarrassed you sound saying that!' He eyed her as though she was a charming curiosity. 'Anyone would think that you had no dealings with the opposite sex.' The grey eyes fixed on her face speculatively.

Suzanne felt her face go hot. Try as she might, she couldn't find any serious recollection of dealings with the opposite sex. Nearly twenty-one and still a virgin. Boyfriends, yes. Her father had always been very indulgent about boyfriends; maybe, she thought now, because he could see that, despite the parties she went to occasionally and the boys she brought back home occasionally, she was still as innocent as a wide-eyed child.

Dane Sutherland had been the only one who had stirred her imagination. Everyone else had been little more than a bit of childish fun. True, when she was nineteen, she had had a fling with a man, someone who had worked with her, but she had never felt that driving passion which she had always associated with a serious affair, and she had not slept with him, despite his persistence. In fact, it had mostly been his persistence that had ended their relationship.

'I've been out with men, yes,' she told him coolly.

'Slept with any of them?'

'That's none of your business.'

'Just curious.' He shrugged and laughed, not at all taken aback by her reply.

'I don't ask you about the women in your life,' Suzanne muttered, irritated as much by his attitude as by his line of questioning.

'Feel free to,' he said, folding his arms and shrugging

again. She caught his eyes and was struck, as she had been years ago, by his magnificent ability to make it seem as though one hundred per cent of his attention was focused entirely on her. A trick of sorts, she knew, a talent for pretence, but how she had once let it work on her. She couldn't think back to her adolescence without cringing.

'I'm not that interested,' she said, wondering whether she should scrape her plate clean or whether that would appear greedy. The food had tasted wonderful—full of tomatoes and herbs. Far better than anything she could whip up. She had never been at her best in a kitchen. Things always seemed to go wrong whenever and wherever they possibly could. Sauces always curdled, or else became lumpy, meat always seemed to burn, and she always managed to forget whatever was boiling until the smell became unavoidable.

She stood up and began clearing away the dishes, vaguely piqued to realise that if she was uninterested in his women then he was even less interested in her response.

He employed, he told her, a woman who came in and cleaned every other day. She also did his ironing and cooked if and when he wanted her to.

'Lucky old you,' she said, watching him as he fixed them cups of coffee and nodded briefly in the direction of the lounge.

'Shall we clear the air, Suzie?' he asked with a resigned sigh. 'Do you dislike me personally, or do you simply dislike the family I represent?'

He sat down on the chair opposite her and stretched out his long legs, crossing them loosely at the ankles.

'How can you expect me to give you an honest answer to that question, when I am not renting a room in your house?'

'Because,' he said steadily, his expression shuttered,

'you haven't yet learned the art of deception. You would like to maintain some kind of dignified coldness, I imagine, but your need to express yourself trips you up constantly. Am I right?'

'You're always right, aren't you?'

'I think that that's one reason why you've let yourself go so utterly for the past few months. You've not spoken to anyone about your father's death. Instead you've bottled up your emotions, which is alien to you, and the result is that you're still as maudlin and confused as you were the day he died.'

'I am neither maudlin nor confused,' she denied hotly.

'You seem to think that I washed my hands of your father the day I left the house,' he said, in a cool statement of fact. 'I did write to him, you know, and a little over a year ago I sent him a cheque in case he needed money. I knew that he had put aside the small legacy my father left him for you. He returned my cheque with a friendly enough letter saying that he was fine.'

Suzanne stared at him, floored by this revelation about which she had known nothing. 'Pride,' she managed to say, recovering her power of speech.

'Almost certainly,' he agreed, either not noticing or else deliberately ignoring the effect that his words had had on her. 'Still, I had no idea that my stepmother was giving him such a hard time.'

'And if you had known, would you have rushed over to save the situation?'

He paused for a fraction of a second—a fraction long enough for her to know that as far as he was concerned he had divorced himself from his past and would not have reopened it willingly. She felt a surge of anger against him and her hand was trembling when she picked up the coffee-cup. He might have offered money to her father, but time was something which he could ill afford to spare.

'I would have dealt with it,' he told her grimly, which did very little to appease her anger.

'From thousands of miles away? How compassionate you are!'

He would have thought about it, she told herself, and written a polite letter, but the urgency of it all would have been lost on him. He had been caught up in a different world and chauffeurs had no place in it. She felt tears of self-pity spring to her eyes, but for once the associated thought of nibbling some chocolate did not arise. She was far too busy feeling angry with him.

'Why have you decided to come back?' she asked. 'If it was so exciting in America, why return?'

'It was now or never.' Five words that silenced her because there was something dark and menacing behind them. 'And you never answered my question,' he said, his features relaxing. 'Do you dislike me personally or do you simply dislike what I represent?'

'Do you care?'

'I'm interested,' he answered lazily, sidestepping the question, which, she knew, had been foolish anyway.

'I don't dislike you,' she said, trying to sound more sophisticated. 'Although, I admit that I don't find your type attractive.'

'And what type is that exactly? Using your vast knowledge of men as a starting point.'

This time she was certain that he was laughing at her. He was a mere nine years older than her but in terms of experience it was tantamount to a lifetime and she knew it. As he did.

'Cruel,' she said, 'arrogant, too good-looking, too cut off from feeling any real emotion about anyone.'

'You have no idea what emotions I feel,' he murmured, sipping some of his coffee and looking at her over the rim of the cup.

She didn't add the real reason that she disliked him—

a dislike that she had nurtured over the years and one that had become more real to her with the passing of time, rather than faded—an overheard conversation, a few passing words before the door closed on her red-faced humiliation.

'You'll have to watch your chauffeur's little girl, Dane.' The merry tinkle of Martha's laughter. She had a way of laughing that made it seem as though she was a vastly superior being. 'She's got a teenage crush on you.'

Suzanne had been hidden from sight, a loose-limbed girl of sixteen on her way to deliver a message from her father.

'Don't concern yourself over that,' Dane had said. His voice had been indifferent, and although she hadn't been able to see him she had imagined him strolling across to the patio doors, looking outside, his thoughts on things that had very little to do with an irritating adolescent and her fanciful illusions.

'But darling,' Martha had said, 'you're a very attractive man—' her voice had been warm and amused '—and a child like that probably finds you irresistible. She peeps at you whenever you're around. You must have noticed that she snatches every opportunity to visit the house when she knows that you're here.'

Dane hadn't answered, and Martha had said, which had been the final blow of mortification, 'Besides, you must remember that she's only the chauffeur's daughter. You mustn't let her get ideas above her station.'

And that had been that. Suzanne had turned away and heard the door shut before she had even made it down the corridor into the hall. The message she had been sent to deliver had flown out of her head completely. It had left a nice, tidy spot, just the right size for her disillusionment to set in.

'And I hold you responsible for the way my father

was treated,' she told him bitterly. 'You may not have been around, but you owed it to the people who worked for your father to see that they were treated properly, instead of just vanishing off the face of the earth and leaving your stepmother in charge. Did you even know that people who had worked for your father for years at the house were dismissed only weeks after your father died?'

She was gathering momentum now and was astounded when he said evenly, betraying no emotion whatever, 'Yes, I did.'

'You...you did?'

'I made sure that they were all financially compensated. Very generously compensated.'

'How on earth did you find out?' Suzanne asked, frowning and trying hard to work out how a man thousands of miles away could have discovered that. Did he have some mysterious crystal ball in his New York penthouse, which he looked into every time he wanted to see what was happening on the other side of the world?

'I have my ways.'

'Spies, you mean?'

'Nothing quite so dramatic.' A shadow of a smile flitted across his dark features. 'Someone there has been keeping an eye on things for me. He told me as soon as Martha began firing old hands.'

'Why didn't you return yourself to sort it out?'

'It would have been impossible.'

Which, to her ears, implied that he hadn't been bothered; but then, if he had been so unbothered, why would he have made sure that his father's men were compensated? Why?

'So you did know about the way Martha treated Dad, then?' she threw at him in an accusing voice, and he shook his head.

'As far as I knew, he was one of the ones who remained in her employment and, as I told you, my offer of money was amicably but firmly returned to sender. I will admit, though, that I was told of...changes, for want of a better word. Certain facts were reported back to me.'

'What facts?'

'Nothing that you need concern yourself with.' His tone of voice did not invite lively debate on the subject. He had thrown her, she thought, a few scraps of information, but he had no intention of explaining any more to her. Probably because he felt no need to launch into any lengthy explanations to a girl who was, after all, beneath him in social standing.

'What did you do with your father's possessions?' he asked suddenly, and she scowled.

'There weren't many. The few big things he had accumulated over the years, I left with a friend in Leamington Spa. I brought the smaller things to London with me.'

She looked down into her coffee-cup. There was a locket with a picture of her mother inside, a stack of old letters which she had written to Santa Claus over the years, and which he had assiduously kept in a scrapbook, all her report cards from school, a box of photographs, the watch which old Mr Sutherland had given to him on his fiftieth birthday and which he had worn every day of his life from the moment he had received it. She had packed them neatly into a small cardboard box and had kept them in her cupboard in the bedsit.

She hoped that he wasn't looking when she wiped a tear away from her cheek. She didn't want him rushing across to her with a load of phoney sympathy and a handkerchief.

'Now,' he said, and there was, thankfully, no indication that he had noticed her brief lapse, 'shall we discuss the job?'

'There's really no need—' she began, thinking that this sounded like a rerun of what she had said when he had offered her a room in his apartment.

'I realise that,' he cut in abruptly. 'Just as I realise what a bitter pill it is for you to swallow, taking anything that's handed to you from a member of my family. But this isn't the act of charity that you'd like to believe. I have several companies over here, all bought with some of my father's inheritance two years ago. I took them over when they were in receivership and they're all now thriving.'

He had bought companies in England after he had moved to America? Why would he have done that? And if he had done that, why bother to go to America at all?

'You've been back to England since you went away?' she asked, perplexed.

'Oh, yes.'

'And still you never came to the house to see your stepmother?'

'No.'

'Why ever not?'

'Don't,' he said with a tinge of impatience, 'ask so many questions.'

'Yes, sir!' she muttered under her breath, and he shot her a crooked smile.

'Good girl. Now, there's a position vacant in one of the companies for an assistant accountant. How far had you reached in your studies?'

Suzanne tucked her feet up underneath her and leant forward, resting her elbows on her knees. Her long hair fell in an untidy tousle of ringlets down the sides of her face and she gave the question some thought.

'I was on the verge of qualification,' she admitted, steeling herself for another fight, but he made no comment, and she explained to him just what she could do, what areas of tax she felt qualified to cover, how knowl-

edgeable she was on company litigation, all the aspects
of audit control which she had found very simple at the
time. While she spoke, he nodded, listening in silence
until she had finished, and she gave a nervous little
laugh.

'Of course, I may have forgotten all of it.'

'I hardly think so. If anything, you're probably over-
qualified for the job I have in mind, but if you were
temping then it'll be more challenging that what you
must have been doing.'

'When it comes to photocopying and filing, most
things pose a greater challenge,' she said with a laugh.
Strange, but it felt as though she hadn't laughed in years.
She could hardly believe that that carefree amused sound
had actually come out of her. And in the company of a
man who sat on the opposite side of the fence to her.

He told her how much she would be paid, and she
looked at him with a fair amount of amazement.

'That's awfully high,' she said at last, and he shook
his head in genuine amusement.

'You will never get far in business if you insist on
being honest to that degree,' he said. 'I pay my workers
well because I want their loyalty and hard work. After
all, they are the backbone of the company and if they're
disgruntled they won't stay. High turnover of staff is
very bad if a company is to succeed.'

'And success is what it's all about.'

'That's right.'

She looked at him frankly. If success was what his
priority was, then he had attained his goal, because it sat
on his shoulders, followed him like a shadow, was there
in the dark look of self-assurance and power.

'Will I be working for you?' she asked suddenly. For
some reason she found the idea of that slightly alarming.
She could cope with bumping into him occasionally in

the apartment, but the prospect of having him around on a more permanent basis made her uneasy.

'Oh, no.' He reached forward and deposited his cup on the table in front of him, then he linked his fingers behind his head and surveyed her. 'I am involved in a company that is quite removed from the one in which you will be working. I leave the running of this particular publishing company in the hands of my directors. They report back to me at frequent intervals.'

'So who is going to be my boss?' Just so long as he bore no resemblance to the odious Mr Slattery then she would be all right.

'A woman by the name of Angela Street. She's American. I sent her over about four months ago when I knew that I would be moving back here. She's smart and efficient and doesn't let the grass grow under her feet.'

A woman? From America? All the way from America when London was full of smart, efficient women?

Who was he trying to kid? She might be naïve but she wasn't born yesterday. Smart, efficient Angela Street was more than a work machine. Why didn't he say so? Why didn't he say that she was his lover?

CHAPTER THREE

WERE clothes for women anything over size ten designed to make them look dull? It appeared so. Suzanne looked at herself in the full-length mirror in the bedroom and decided that she looked frumpy. She had worn the suit for two months without that thought ever crossing her mind, but it crossed it now, and she tried, without much success, to smooth the skirt into a semblance of something chic.

It was a light summer suit but the colours were insipid and the overall grey effect didn't do much for her.

She had tied her long, unruly hair back into a French plait which hung down her back, but strands kept escaping and short of gluing them to the side of her head there seemed little she could do to avoid it.

It was, all things considered, just as well that Dane wasn't around. He was out of the country for a few days. He wouldn't have said anything about her appearance but those cool, assessing grey eyes would have said it on his behalf anyway and she would have instantly retreated into a position of muted self-defence, which was childish, she knew, but which was something she couldn't seem to prevent.

He had, he had told her, spoken to Angela and there was nothing to be nervous about.

'Why on earth should I be nervous?' she had asked him airily. 'Does she bite?'

'Nothing quite so dramatic,' he had answered drily,

his eyes resting on her and making her feel hot and bothered, and cross to be feeling that way. 'But she's extremely capable and quite intolerant of temper tantrums.'

'I did not lose my last job because of a temper tantrum,' Suzanne had told him hotly, but she was uncomfortably aware that her outspokenness to her last boss, justified though it had been, had stepped beyond the lines of good sense.

At the time she hadn't cared. She hadn't enjoyed the job, she had been paid a pittance and she had had no real idea of why she had stuck the damn thing out for so long, apart from the fact that it had been convenient.

She found now that she cared a great deal about keeping this job. It might have been a charitable handout to assuage Dane Sutherland's guilty conscience, it might have been offered out of remembered affection for her father and the daughter who had harboured a teenage crush on him, but she wasn't about to live down to his expectations of her as a child by jeopardising it in any way.

She looked at the photograph of her father, which she had put on the dressing table, and for once she found that her eyes did not automatically fill with tears. She told the picture of the middle-aged man with the kind eyes and the self-conscious expression of someone posing for the camera that her personal dislike of Dane Sutherland wasn't going to get in the way of doing a good job.

'He won't be able to think, even for a fleeting second, that I failed the test and what else could you expect of the chauffeur's daughter.' Her voice echoed in the silence of the room and she grinned and wondered whether she was going mad. Talking to photographs. What next?

The company was one of four that Dane had bought over the three years that he had been away and hauled out of the doldrums, back into mainstream life.

It was, she discovered as she stood in front of it later, larger than she had anticipated. For the first time she acknowledged a certain nervousness underneath the defiant desire to succeed.

She had expected something altogether smaller—a little building, in need of renovation because of its slow decline into debt. She hadn't realised quite how drastic its kiss of life had been.

The office block was a large, three-storeyed building which seemed to consist mostly of glass—smoky-grey glass. There was a stream of people hurrying in. Suzanne stood for a while in the cool summer sunshine and watched the figures being absorbed one by one into the bowels of the glass building; then she took a deep breath and joined the throng.

She had brought her briefcase with her, partly so that she could carry in a couple of accountancy books and one law one, and partly because the briefcase had been given to her by her father as a present and she wouldn't have dreamt of going into any job without it, even if the job had involved manual labour on a building site. It was her good-luck charm.

She laid it protectively on her lap as she sat in the reception room and waited to be summoned.

It was, she thought, very American in its decor, or perhaps the places where she had worked before—small, fairly stuffy offices—were just very English in their shabbiness.

There was a feeling of space and light and a great many plants everywhere. The three large paintings on the wall were all abstract, their colours strong and defined, red, orange and blue lines that swept across the canvases, conveying a message which, Suzanne thought, was lost on her. She personally preferred paintings

which contained things that were recognisable—scenes
of mountains or lakes or forests which seduced you into
closing your eyes and imagining that you were far away
from the hustle and bustle of the twentieth century.

To the far right from where she was sitting was a bank
of four lifts. Angela Street, she thought, would emerge
from one of those, and reluctantly she allowed herself to
give free rein to the curiosity which had been gnawing
away at her ever since she had drawn her conclusions
on Dane's relationship with Angela.

She had told herself that it was pointless speculating
on the American, because she really couldn't care one
way or another whether he was sleeping with her, pro-
posing to marry her, or even planning a brood of mini-
ature Dane Sutherlands, but still she wondered what the
other woman was like.

Would she be like the girls he used to bring back to
the house? Small and pretty and with smiling, awed eyes
that followed him around wherever he went?

Suzanne had observed them all from a distance, occasionally hearing more about them from her brother
who had found it all wildly exciting, and she had hated
them all.

She was still absorbed in her trip down memory lane
when she saw a mousy-haired girl with earnest eyes ap-
proaching her, and she stood up and held out her hand.

'Miss Street?' she asked hesitantly, and the girl's pale,
thin face broke into a smile.

'One of Miss Street's secretaries,' she explained, leading the way to the lift while Suzanne followed in her
wake. 'And she likes to be called Angela, by the way.
She says that there shouldn't be barriers between boss
and secretary.'

Suzanne clutched her briefcase by the handle and nodded. 'Did you find your way here all right?' the girl
asked—her name, it transpired, was Emma—and Suz-

anne smiled again and nodded and made polite conversation as the lift took them to the top floor and disgorged them into a corridor which was plushly carpeted and exuded that indefinable quality of something recently refurbished with no expense spared.

It gave the illusion of being open-plan and it was only on closer inspection that you realised that although the secretaries were visible, industriously working away or walking along the corridor with a sense of purpose, the hierarchy were not. Their offices were set further back so that you had to stop and peer beyond the outer offices to see the more exclusive ones behind.

It was, however, quite a change from the last place she had worked, where there had been a great deal of milling around and an overall impression of barely restrained chaos.

'It's very quiet,' Suzanne said to her companion. 'I feel as though I'm in a library.'

She received a sympathetic grin back. 'There is a library, as a matter of fact—just a small one at the end of the building. The silence in there makes this floor look like Piccadilly Circus in comparison. Angela doesn't mind us talking, but she says that constant chatting is disruptive to an efficient business.'

By the time they had reached the very last office at the end Suzanne had added a few more impressions of Dane's mistress to her list, because mistress was what she undoubtedly was. A logical process of deduction had told her so, even if Dane had not.

But nothing had prepared her for the woman sitting behind the huge desk.

Emma had closed the door behind her and Suzanne stood and looked at Angela Street, who was on the telephone and only briefly glanced up to point to the chair facing her, then returned to her conversation.

She was, Suzanne thought, the most beautiful woman she had ever seen.

She looked as though she was in her mid-thirties, but her skin was flawless and honey-coloured and her short blonde hair was very precisely tailored so that it framed her face—thick and straight and with the rich, creamy shades of the natural blonde.

She finished whatever high-level conversation she had been conducting, stood up and held out her hand, and next to her Suzanne felt like a towering, overweight Amazon.

'I'm Angela,' she said, her green eyes hard and efficient. 'Please, sit down.'

There's something about her, Suzanne thought, uncomfortably aware that she was being uncharitable, that I don't like. Was it the fact that the beautiful face seemed hard and lacking in anything that was vulnerable? Or maybe it was the eyes, which looked as though they assessed and didn't forgive easily what they didn't like.

'Now,' she said, 'I'm not sure what Dane has told you about the company, so you'll have to stop me if I'm repeating information, but let me explain just what we do here.'

Suzanne thought that she would probably be decapitated if she stopped the other woman in mid-flow and told her that she was repeating things. Angela Street didn't look like the kind of person who liked being interrupted.

So she listened in polite silence to the crisp American accent and tried to stifle her uneasy feeling that this woman was not to be trusted, though she had to admit that she was probably being petty. How could you dislike someone after half an hour?

She could also, reluctantly, and with an odd feeling of resentment, see exactly why Dane had imported her all the way from America. She had that unusual combination, like him, of great intelligence and great beauty. She listened to the monologue on company performance, with its implied message that most of its success was due to policies introduced by the speaker, and pictured Dane with the blonde, the stares they would get. They were, she imagined, the perfect couple. One small and blonde and exquisitely beautiful, the other tall and dark and sinfully handsome. They would discuss high finance and business trends and he wouldn't treat her like a simpleton who needed taking care of.

'Now,' Angela said, looking down at her watch, 'have you any questions?'

Suzanne asked a few and hoped that she sounded more intelligent than she felt.

She would be working, she was told, in the office alongside this one, and would refer all enquiries to her.

'Mr Sutherland—Dane—has nothing whatsoever to do with this company. He has entrusted the running of it entirely to me.' Angela linked her fingers together, leant forward and said, without preamble, 'This is a very unusual situation, Suzanne, and I can't pretend that I was happy about having you here. I am very much against nepotism of any sort. Dane has explained to me how sorry he felt for you and that he felt more or less obliged to give you a job. He thought that working for me would do you a great deal of good.'

Suzanne listened to this and tried to keep the polite smile rigidly fixed on her lips. Sorry for me? Obliged to give me a job? she thought.

'It appears,' Angela continued, her mouth a narrow line and her eyes unsmiling, 'that he feels somewhat responsible for you because he knew you at some point in time. However, don't think that this affords you any special treatment within this organisation.'

'I don't,' Suzanne said, her face aching from the effort of the continual smile.

'I also—and I feel that we should discuss this quite openly because I don't believe in hiding things—do not think that it's entirely appropriate that you should be sharing his apartment.'

She waited for a response and Suzanne didn't volunteer one, so she continued with a slightly harder inflection in her voice. 'You're a young girl and I'm sure you don't like the restraints imposed in sharing his place, do you? I've explained this to Dane, and we both agree that it would probably be better for you if you made an attempt to find your own place—once you've settled down here, naturally.' She spoke as though she and Dane were a couple, two lovebirds sharing their every thought, and it was all Suzanne could do not to ask exactly what the relationship was.

'Dane never mentioned that to me!' Suzanne said, stricken. 'Of course, I had no intention of outstaying my welcome.'

Angela smiled. 'Of course not. A child like you wants to be able to bring boyfriends back in privacy.'

'Boyfriends? I haven't got any boyfriends.'

Angela stood up. 'You will,' she said, with a show of womanly camaraderie which Suzanne didn't join in. 'I remember being your age and all the excitement of boys and clothes and parties.' Suzanne found it hard to imagine Angela Street giggling over boys and getting drunk at parties. She didn't seem the type somehow. 'I'm sure that you'll see quite a bit of me around and I guess that Dane and I will seem very stuffy to you. Two old fogies!'

'Why would I see a lot of you around?' she asked innocently.

'Because we work closely together and have a lot in common.' Angela's voice was sharp.

'I'm sorry to appear rude, but I had no idea that you

two were involved. Dane mentioned nothing of this to me.'

Was it her imagination or was there a flicker of something that crossed that beautiful, marble-smooth face?

'He can be very private,' Angela said quickly. 'It's not in my nature, I'm afraid, to discuss personal matters with my staff. I shall simply leave it to your imagination. Although—' manufactured warmth replaced the coldness '—you're so young that your imagination is probably far too occupied with your own personal matters!'

Suzanne was tempted to point out that he was hardly that much older than she was herself, but she bit back the words. She had an instinctive feeling that any such remark would fall neatly into the category of tactlessness, and look at what happened to the last job when tactlessness had got the better of her.

'Now, I'm sorry to have to run, but I have a very important meeting with potential clients in an hour's time.' Angela gave the impression of having other things on her mind now that this little matter had been dealt with, and Suzanne hastily got to her feet and walked towards the door.

The feeling of being huge and somehow clumsy swept over her again as she shook hands with Angela. She had never really regretted being tall, but right now she did wish that she were a couple of inches shorter so that she didn't have to look down at the compact blonde woman with her diamond-hard, beautiful eyes.

Angela deposited her at her office, which she was sharing with the other assistant accountant, a young man about her own age with red hair, freckles and a face that looked as though it was on the brink of breaking into a grin.

'Robert will show you the ropes,' Angela said, frowning at the cigarette in the ashtray, which was happily burning away.

'She would like me to give up the evil habit,' Robert said to Suzanne cheerily, once their door was closed. 'I've even been sent on a course but I'm stoutly refusing. I hope you don't mind. I actually don't smoke very many, but the unfortunate thing is that every time she walks in I seem to be in the middle of one.'

Suzanne immediately felt at home. 'Unlucky, that,' she agreed, grinning, and they companionably settled into work, with Robert painstakingly going through files with her, showing her charts and graphs and figures, which she grasped fairly instantly, much to her relief.

There was far more breadth to the job than there had been to those in the two companies in which she had previously worked. Her involvement stretched way beyond the limits of accountancy and seemed to incorporate much of everything. She assumed that this was because there was no old order which rigidly defined jobs and laid down guidelines that were impossible to over-step.

And she had to admit that, dislikeable though the woman was, Angela Street was competent. She had done more than simply set up the company. She had brought in new work and her involvement in some of the tax problems showed that her knowledge was far wider than was usual in a financial accountant.

I should respect her, Suzanne thought to herself later that evening as she settled down in front of the televi-sion. She's undoubtedly a brilliant worker. And so beau-tiful as well. Her looks alone must be in her favour when it comes to winning clients. How could anyone ignore that face?

Suzanne looked down at the hearty meal that she had prepared for herself, having taken her time because Dane wasn't around, and wouldn't be for the next few days, and relished the pleasure of a big kitchen, which had gadgets and devices in it that actually did what they were supposed to do.

For once she had felt inclined to stay away from her normal unhealthy diet of a hamburger and chips, or a bowl of cereal if she really was in no mood to do anything at all, and had made herself a pasta dish which included quite a bit of cream. It didn't really resemble the picture in the recipe book—one of her father's birthday presents to her because, he had laughingly told her, she'd end up making someone an absolutely horrendous wife if the thought of pots and pans brought her out in a cold sweat. She had omitted one or two of the ingredients and added a couple of her own, but it smelt good.

She thought of Angela's sylph-like figure, took two mouthfuls and regretfully shoved the remainder aside.

Something in her had shifted—an awareness of herself—and for the first time since her father had died she seemed to rediscover the determination which had brought her to London and which had vanished somewhere along the way. She even resisted the bar of chocolate while she watched television.

Angela, she thought, had cleverly managed to convey a number of things to her during that interview, in not so many words. She had managed to say, without really spelling it out, that Suzanne was immature, that she was seen by Dane as an object of pity, that her presence in the flat was an impediment to a relationship which she didn't put into words but succeeded in implying all the same, never mind all her fine words about Suzanne needing her own space to bring her own boyfriends round for visits.

The general upshot had been that the apartment was no longer a haven for the two of them because she, Suzanne, would be around—an unwelcome, unsightly blot on the landscape. And what really infuriated her was that

Dane agreed with all this. Why would the other woman lie?

It was just as well that he was absent from the scene. The few days' reprieve would give her time to control her wayward temper.

But she wasn't going to shower him with servile gratitude, and if that was what he was waiting for then he would simply have to wait until hell froze over. She had been rescued, true enough, from joblessness and penury, but she didn't like her rescuer and if her circumstances hadn't been so dire she would have happily rejected his offers without a second thought.

And, besides, she found after two days that she was beginning rather to enjoy working for the company.

She had abandoned accountancy because she had been unsure that it was what she had wanted, yet slowly a liking for it was creeping over her. She couldn't explain it; she could only assume that this was because the job was so varied.

She saw next to nothing of Angela, whose infrequent visits appeared to be along the lines of checking up to make sure work was being done rather than giving encouragement, and that suited her just fine. She disliked the bright smile with its rows of perfect pearl-white teeth, she disliked that crisp voice that somehow implied that Angela was a cut above the rest of the human race.

And Robert was a dream to work with. He was bright, capable and endlessly amusing on the subject of his girlfriend. He also left her in complete control of her accounts, and the responsibility, she discovered, agreed with her.

It was fun being on the inside of a newly developing company, where there was always scope for input and where the new was not necessarily the bad.

Two days later she was sitting at her desk, eating an apple because she no longer seemed to have the time to indulge in anything more substantial if it meant taking her out of the office for any length of time, when the door opened.

She didn't look up. It would be Robert, returning, no doubt, crestfallen after an unsuccessful lunch with Annie. It seemed to be the pattern of their relationship: arguments, followed by ecstatic reconciliations, followed by yet more arguments, a never-ending road which they both seemed to quietly enjoy walking down. After only a few days Suzanne felt as though she had known them both for years.

'Hello.' The cool, deep voice made her head swing up. 'Just thought that I'd look in and see how you're getting along.'

Somehow, she hadn't expected to see him here. Come to it, she hadn't really expected to see him anywhere at all, at least not for another few days, and the surprise of him lounging against the doorframe in his charcoal-grey suit made her flush.

'Fine, thank you.' She half rose to her feet and then sat back down, feeling clumsy and awkward.

Angela approached and slipped next to him, linking her hand lightly through his arm—a gesture of ownership which he hardly appeared to notice.

I was right, Suzanne thought; they do look good together.

'We're going out to lunch,' Angela said, which was the first time that she had volunteered any information as to her whereabouts, apart from briefly leaving her mobile-telephone number in case she was urgently needed back at the office. Presumably the mobile phone wasn't going to be making up a threesome on this particular occasion.

'Fine.' Suzanne avoided looking at Dane. The anger she had put aside over the past few days was threatening to break its leash. If he hadn't wanted to let her use his apartment, then it would only have been fair to make that clear at the beginning. She hadn't asked for his charity, had she?

'You're not spending your lunch-hour in here, are you?' Dane asked, his grey eyes focusing on her with amused surprise.

'I do keep telling her,' Angela said, answering the question on Suzanne's behalf, 'that she should stretch her legs and go outside but she prefers to work through her lunch.'

This was the first time any such concern had been expressed about her needing to stretch her legs. For the past four days Angela had been more than happy to have her man the telephones in an empty office.

'The exercise would do you good,' Angela said in a sweetly caring voice which made Suzanne's teeth snap together in irritation. She certainly knew how to drop the hard-as-nails image when it suited her.

'Why don't you join us?' Dane asked. 'We're heading off for a quick Italian in Covent Garden.'

'No.' The thought of being an unwanted third party with the two of them was enough to bring on a heart attack. 'I mean no, thank you. I have quite a bit of work here I'd like to finish.'

'Yes, Dane,' Angela said quickly, 'we mustn't drag the poor child out if she's intent on doing her work. It's not often we see such dedication in the young, is it?'

Dane ignored her. 'Come on,' he said. 'You can finish that work later.'

Suzanne didn't know whether the prospect of lunch for three was more appalling for her or for Angela. The other woman's face had certainly set into granite hardness.

So she reluctantly followed them into the lift, noticing that he had shrugged off the hand on his arm and was clearly not into public demonstrations of affection, because he was standing on the opposite side to Angela and making no move to close the gap.

'And how does the work compare to what you were doing in Warwick?' Dane asked, addressing her for the first time when they had stepped into the taxi.

'It's very interesting,' Suzanne began, reluctantly meeting those mesmerising eyes and trying not to feel diminished by Angela, whose legs were gracefully crossed, exposing just the right amount of thigh beneath the jade-green, short silk shirt.

'Yes, your last job was in a very small company, wasn't it?' Angela asked, shifting her position slightly so that slightly more bare thigh was exposed.

'Quite small, yes, but—'

'I did initially wonder—' Angela looked up at Dane with a conspiratorial smile '—whether Suzanne would be able to cope. After all, a family firm is such a different kettle of fish, isn't it? But she's doing marvellously well.'

'Thank you. But my last company was—'

'Now,' Angela said, eliminating Suzanne entirely from her range of vision, 'Dane, tell me all about the trip. How was New York?' Back to the efficient, career-woman voice, Suzanne noticed.

'Still standing,' Dane drawled wryly, looking across to Suzanne, who promptly stared out of the window. This situation was beginning to remind her unpleasantly of when she had been much younger, when she would accidentally meet him with one of his girlfriends and be reduced in a matter of minutes to feeling clumsy and gauche and virtually on another planet altogether. Although, it had to be said that he had been more physical with his girlfriends then than now.

'Who did you meet?' Angela pressed. 'Did you see

Bruce? I had a fax from him two days ago. The acquisition you were working on has gone through, I take it?'

'We don't want to discuss work-related matters now, do we?' Dane asked in a voice that expected no debate on the subject.

'Please,' Suzanne said, turning to them, 'don't mind me. I'm happy to just enjoy the passing scenery. I don't often get the unexpected pleasure of being taken for a drive.'

If you see me as a charity case, she thought acidly, then I might just as well oblige by acting like one, and Dane looked at her with a frown.

'I find it's the only way to get around London,' Angela said. 'The underground is so grimy.'

'I like it,' Suzanne said. 'It's a bit claustrophobic during the rush hour but—'

'I think it's far easier to bear those throngs of people when you're younger.' Angela pouted at Dane. 'Don't you agree, Dane? Not that I'm an old woman—' she laughed and ran her fingers through her hair with a graceful movement '—but I can't bear being surrounded by too many people. I guess...' she laughed again—a surprised laugh as though she was only now coming to this revealing conclusion '...it's because I grew up in one of those traditional three-car households in America and I hardly knew the meaning of public transport.'

'I didn't think that there was such a thing as a traditional three-car household,' Suzanne said politely. She longed to be back at her desk with only her apple for company.

'It comes as something of a surprise to me as well,' Dane said with a laugh.

And Angela obviously felt that she had somehow been pushed to the fringe, because she said in a tighter voice, 'I suppose "traditional" isn't quite the word. I suppose I don't like to boast about my upbringing, which was a very privileged one.' She murmured to Dane, 'You must share the feeling.'

Now Suzanne could see well enough where the conversation had been leading. Angela must have known that her father was no more than a chauffeur, a hired hand, employed to serve Dane's family, and she had been making sure that the message was fully understood.

You might have been given a job and a room, Angela was telling her, but don't let it go to your head. You're a child, and, moreover, one from a different background—the wrong background. He felt sorry for you, but just remember the differences.

What else had he told her? Suzanne wondered angrily.

'Not really,' Dane said coolly as the taxi dropped them outside the restaurant.

'I guess not,' Angela said under her breath standing beside him at the entrance. 'I admire that. I can't bear snobs.'

From behind them, feeling rather distanced and hulkish, Suzanne looked at the small blonde and wondered what it would be like if she missed her footing and fell with an almighty crash to the pavement, landing in a spectacularly ungraceful position. She stuck her hands behind her back just in case the temptation to help fate along with a little push overcame her.

It didn't seem fair that she shouldn't at least bury her wretchedness under some creamy food, but she had salad and pretended not to notice Dane's raised eyebrows at the order.

It was only when, after the meal had finished, Angela took herself off to the Ladies that Dane turned to her and said bluntly, 'What the hell is the matter with you, Suzie? You can't be finding the job that great. You look bloody miserable.'

Oh, thank you very much, she thought sourly, for the compliment of a lifetime.

'I love the job,' she said back at him, two spots of colour on her cheeks. 'What I don't love is the fact that you sent Angela Street along to do your dirty work!'

'What the hell are you on about now?'

'You know what I'm on about!'

'I am not telepathic and I have no idea what you're talking about, and quite frankly I am not in the mood to play some kind of elaborate guessing game with you. If you have something to say, why don't you just say it instead of taking refuge behind sulks?'

'I have not been sulking!'

'No? You barely said a word during lunch and when one of us asked you anything you answered in mono-syllables. That seems to me to be a pretty accurate de-scription of someone sulking.'

'All right! I admit that I didn't feel particularly thrilled to be included in your little lunch rendezvous. It may have escaped your notice but Angela was less than im-pressed when you asked me to tag along!'

'Rendezvous? What on earth are you on about now? Your imagination is running away with you. It seems to be something of a habit.' He drank the remainder of his gin and tonic and regarded her with amusement as he put the glass down in front of him.

Suzanne went on, 'You can't be that much in touch with women if you didn't notice how much Angela re-sented my presence here today. She expected to have you to herself and instead she found herself lumbered with a party of three.'

'Have me to herself? She may have been a bit taken aback because there were certain aspects of my trip she wanted to discuss, but that's about it.'

'Oh, is that a fact?' Suzanne muttered, head bent, con-fused and embarrassed. When she raised her head, it was to find him grinning at her.

'Because you had a crush on me doesn't mean that the entire female race is bowled over by my charm.'

'I do not have a crush on you!' She was so mortified that she could hardly speak.

'*Had.*' He was still grinning and looking thoroughly entertained. 'Past tense. You forgot that you've already told me how much you dislike me and how immune you are to my particular species. Arrogant, I believe you said; too good-looking, too full of myself.'

Suzanne spluttered.

'I'm probably misreading the whole situation, though,' he said thoughtfully, rubbing his chin with his long fingers, then shooting her a look from under his lashes. 'Perhaps you're feeling a little edgy because your self-esteem just lately has taken a beating, and it's left you vulnerable to feeling a certain amount of jealousy for Angela. She is, I suppose, a very beautiful woman.'

Which, she finished to herself for him, is something you're never likely to be. Her father had thought that she was beautiful, but that had been paternal affection talking. She was too tall, too vivid ever to be classed as beautiful. At her very best, and before she had put on weight, she had occasionally thought herself attractive, but real beauty was like Angela's—a face that was carved into perfection, with hair that hung like a glossy curtain at the side of her face instead of rebelling against all restraints and demanding attention.

He signalled to the waiter but kept his eyes on her face. 'Have I hit the nail on the head, Suzie?'

'You have not! In fact, you're so far off target that you need your eyes tested!' But her objections seemed hollow and a little overheated. 'It's just that Angela seems to know the full extent of why I'm working for her—'

'Should it have been a secret?'

'—and I don't care to be discussed behind my back.'

'I'm getting a little tired of your puerile outrage over every little thing—'

'*Every little thing!* You think it's nice to know that you've been telling the whole world how sorry you feel for me, how you felt morally obliged to offer me a roof over my head and an income until something better came along?'

'You're trying my patience...'

'My humblest apologies.' She leant forward. 'But I do feel it would be better if I found, at least, somewhere else to live, don't you?'

Angela had emerged from the Ladies.

'This,' he countered, all amusement gone, leaning forward as well so that he was far too close to her for her liking, 'is neither the time nor the place to discuss this. We'll talk about it later. In the apartment. I'll be home at eight. By which time I trust that you'll have your unruly temper in check.'

CHAPTER FOUR

SUZANNE had planned to just mention it all very casually.

'Angela,' she had planned to say, in passing and more or less over one shoulder, 'has mentioned that it might be a good idea if I start looking around for a flat as soon as possible. I'm very grateful for your putting me up, but I agree with her, and I'll start trying to find somewhere as soon as possible.'

No more outbursts, no childish hints at his relationship with Angela, whatever that might be. Cool, calm and collected. Three qualities, which seemed conspicuous by their absence whenever he was around, but which she had to lay her hands on somewhere if she weren't to be the constant butt of his infuriating amusement at her expense.

Of course, she should have casually mentioned it at the restaurant at lunchtime, just as she should have casually omitted that Angela had had anything to do with her decision, but as usual he had managed to throw her off course.

Now the whole thing had escalated, at least in her mind, to the point of confrontation, and at seven-thirty she found herself sitting in her bedroom, with the television on, looking at the clock every three minutes.

He came home before eight. She knew that because she heard his movements through her closed door. At eight-thirty she sauntered out in her jeans and white shirt and adopted an air of complete surprise when she found him in the kitchen making himself a cup of coffee.

He had taken off his jacket, which was draped over the back of a chair, and had rolled his striped shirt up to the elbows.

'I wondered whether you were in,' he said, leaning against the kitchen counter and looking at her. 'There's no need to hide yourself away in your bedroom, you know.'

'Oh, I wasn't hiding myself away.' She sat down at the kitchen table and folded her arms. 'I quite like it, actually. I read, watch the television; it's restful.'

'Someone of your age shouldn't be having restful evenings, surely?' He laughed—a low, throaty laugh that made her resolve to be perfectly relaxed and controlled slip a little.

'And what should someone of my age be doing?' she asked innocently. 'Inviting little chums to tea, followed by some children's television and colouring?'

'Sarcasm doesn't become you.' He sat down opposite her with his cup of coffee and looked at her steadily.

'I wasn't being sarcastic. I'm just reacting against your constant implications that I'm young enough to be your daughter. I'm nearly twenty-one and I stopped colouring and playing with my painting set a long time ago.'

'I know you're not a child, Suzie,' he murmured, and his eyes followed her ample curves in a way that made the blood rush to her head. 'I would have to be blind not to see that you're no longer the lanky, flat-chested girl who used to come running whenever I called.'

Suzanne felt her breathing begin to get a bit thick. No, definitely not flat-chested. Her full breasts were hardly ever contained in a bra when she was at home. She could feel them hanging now, like ripe fruit.

'Then stop treating me like a child. You arrived on

my doorstep unannounced, informed me that I was incapable of looking after myself, carted me off here, manufactured a job for me working for your imported managing director, probably because you thought that it would do me good—' She had very nearly said that that was what Angela had told her at any rate. 'And you expect me not to accuse you of treating me as though I had lost my wits somewhere along the line?'

His eyes narrowed. 'We've been through most of this before and I don't intend to go into it again. You've decided to interpret my actions in the way that suits your argument, and that's fine, but spare me the outbursts.'

If she had been holding a cup, she would have slammed it on the table. In the absence of one, she slammed her open hand on the table, palm down, which hurt, and said angrily, 'Do you deny that there's some truth in what I've said?'

'You make it sound as though I'm the big, bad wolf. Why don't you try looking at the truth a little more dispassionately, if you can do that?' The temperature of his voice was dropping by degrees by the minute and she could tell that he wasn't too impressed with her outburst. He had never been a great one for showing great explosions of feeling, and he disliked it in other people, she assumed, but wasn't that just too bad?

'And what is the truth? According to Dane Sutherland.'

'The truth is that you had completely given up on everything. You were living in a bedsit which was only just short of needing demolition, you had just lost your job, which from the sounds of it was hardly worth having in the first place, and the bald truth of the matter was that you didn't have a clue what to do next.'

'I was happy being clueless!' She stood up and leant on her hands against the top of the table. She felt as though in a minute she would be breathing fire.

'You were miserable!' He wasn't shouting, but his voice was clear and hard and she felt a strange pleasure as she watched his initial impatience develop into anger.

'So you felt a little conscience-stricken and decided to take me away from all that! I only came with you because I had no choice!'

'You came with me because you wanted to,' he ground out. 'If you've managed to convince yourself that I dragged you here kicking and screaming all the way, then you're a fool!'

'So I'm a fool now, on top of everything else!'

He stood up and leant towards her, so that their positions were mirrored, but with the width of the table separating them, which was just as well because he looked as though he wanted to hit her.

She only realised that, leaning over as she was, her shirt was gaping at the front, exposing her breasts to him when she saw his eyes glance down, and then he straightened up and walked towards the kitchen sink. He stood there, with his back to her, and she hurriedly did up one of the buttons, horrified at the thought that he had seen everything.

Her face was still pink when he eventually turned around to face her and leant against the sink, his hands in his pockets, his feet loosely crossed at the ankles.

'No, you're not a fool, Suzie Stanton. Anything but.' They stared at each other. The overhead light was harsh and it made the planes and angles of his face seem even harsher.

If she had stopped and thought about it, she would have just found somewhere else and left, without flinging accusations at him, but she hadn't been thinking straight. It seemed to be a problem for her whenever he was around.

There was a long silence between them. 'Have you eaten tonight?' he asked, and she nodded.

'A salad.'

'Another salad?'

He was trying to lighten the atmosphere. Had he felt the same thing that she had? That sudden shift into dangerous, unknown waters?

'I'm trying to lose some weight. I think I've told you that before.'

'There's such a thing as being too thin.'

'Is there? Not according to most fashion magazines. Or most clothes shops, come to that.'

There was something brittle about their conversation and she was relieved when he took those watchful eyes off her and she could sit back down, rather shakily.

'Look,' she began, tracing patterns on the table with her finger, 'I'm not sulking, or being childish, but I'm old enough to realise that my presence here might pose a problem for you.'

'In what way?'

'You're being deliberately obtuse. You have a personal life. I'm not a complete fool. And I know that my presence here will eventually get in the way of that personal life. If it hasn't already.' She wasn't going to mention Angela. She was sick of getting mixed messages. Was he sleeping with her or wasn't he? Angela implied that there was something there—something rather more than the boss and his faithful worker. She was sick of it gnawing away at the back of her mind like a persistent little parasite that wouldn't give up.

'Don't concern yourself with my personal life. Do I concern myself with yours?' His voice was mild, but his eyes had an amused glitter in them. Personal life? she wanted to say. Children don't *have* personal lives, do they?

'You will tell me, though, the minute you want me out, won't you?' she said grudgingly. 'Not that I intend making this an indefinite stay, but I won't rush into another place which should be condemned, if I don't have to.'

'Very wise.'

She threw him a watery smile and stood up. Confrontation over. Time to return to her bedroom, where she felt much more comfortable anyway. He might find it perfectly acceptable for her to wander around as though she owned the place, but she didn't and she wasn't about to abuse his hospitality. More to the point, he didn't find himself thrown into confusion every time she walked in, did he? Whereas, Suzanne thought in a muddled way, her mind started wandering whenever he was around.

'Going so soon?' he asked softly as she walked past him, and she stopped to look at him.

'Well, I did only come in so that we could discuss this...this matter.'

'And what are you going to do in your bedroom that's so important?' he asked.

'Finish my book,' she answered.

'Sounds exciting.' There was lazy charm in his voice and she should have been alarmed and cautious at that, but she had never been able to resist him when he was in this mood and she was finding it very difficult to do it now. 'Come into the sitting room and talk to me instead. It's been one hell of a week.'

'And you could do with falling asleep to my boring conversation?' But she wasn't waspish when she said that and he laughed under his breath.

'No,' he said slowly, pushing himself away from the counter and walking into the sitting room, while she followed him, 'I wouldn't say that there was anything about you that is boring. Tempestuous, maybe, but not boring.'

He sat down on the sofa with his arm outstretched along the back, and she sat down on one of the chairs facing him, tucking her legs up under her. She had tied her hair back into a pony-tail, but it was spilling about everywhere, and she reached back and unclasped it, shaking her head so that it fell in its usual disorderly mass over her shoulders.

'Why has it been a bad week?' she asked politely, and he rested his head on the back of the sofa and closed his eyes. Like that, she could see that he was tired.

'I'm in the middle of investigating a possible acquisition,' he said, without opening his eyes, 'and it's a very delicate one. Every step has to be made carefully. Very wearying.'

'You mean you prefer to charge in there, blowing horns and making your presence felt.'

'If I'm taking over a company, I like it to be a direct manoeuvre. Right now, I'm conducting a sort of dance, having to make sure that everything goes very slowly.' He opened his eyes and looked at her. 'Did you see much of Martha when you were still living at home?' he asked, and she frowned, puzzled at the question.

'Only if it was unavoidable,' Suzanne told him bluntly. 'I realise that she's a part of your family, even if you aren't blood-related, but I had nothing in common with her.'

If they had been the same age and had met, she thought, as teenagers, she still wouldn't have had anything in common with her. Suzanne had been a tomboy as a child, had always preferred the freedom of casual clothes, rarely wore anything that matched. She would start off with good intentions, but somewhere along the line, usually by the time she got to her feet, she would find herself running late and would spoil whatever effect she had created by wearing the wrong shoes. Martha had been an impeccable dresser. That seemed, to her, to sum up the essential difference between them.

'Apart from what was going on at the house,' Dane said, his voice still easy and offhand, 'what else was happening there?'

'In the village, you mean?' Suzanne was becoming more bewildered. She felt that underneath the bland, general questions he was asking her something very directly, but what that something was she had no idea.

'The usual,' she said. Was he really interested in little local scandals? If he was, he would have returned back at least once, wouldn't he? 'A few births, a few deaths, a few rows between neighbours. Stanley Cooper's wife ran off with his neighbour. Mary Deacon's daughter had a baby and no one ever found out who the father was.' Suzanne grinned at that because Mary Deacon had always been very self-righteous when it had come to other people's morals. There had been a good deal of sniggering when the unthinkable had happened to her daughter.

'Nothing else?' he asked, and she shook her head. 'And don't you miss all that? The peace and tranquillity? Village life where a little local scandal keeps everyone happy?'

She felt her hackles rise a little at what she interpreted as criticism.

'London is a good experience,' she said defensively. 'It was different when my father was alive. All that meant a lot more then.' She realised, with a start of surprise, that she didn't feel the pain and anger that had plagued her for months at the mention of her father.

'And are the bright lights going to keep you here or are you going to get fed up?'

'Are you worried that I might run out on the job you very kindly provided for me?' Suzanne asked, wondering how she could ever have been lulled into feeling any kind of companionship with this man.

'Did I say that?'

'You didn't have to. I can read between the lines as well as anybody else. And you can rest assured that I have no plans for returning home. Not,' she laughed bitterly, 'that there's any home left to return to.'

'So we're back to this, are we?' His voice was sharp, impatient, and she realised with a little dismay that they had resumed their fighting stances once again. It was hard to think that there had been a time when there was no animosity between them. But then everything had been different then and there was no point in making comparisons between the past and the present. The present was all that mattered.

'I'm sorry,' she said insincerely. 'I forgot that I was under orders not to mention that again.' Which only made his eyes narrow further. 'In a minute I suppose you'll tell me that I'm acting like a child.' Which would only be echoing, she thought, what Angela implied at every given opportunity. 'Do you think that big, bad London is a little too grown-up for me?' she pressed, feeling as though she was back on the steamroller and unable to get off now that she had started.

'Maybe that's what you think,' he answered smoothly. 'Although, you did look like a lost, abandoned little girl when I saw you for the first time in that bedsit.'

He wasn't being unkind when he said it but she didn't appreciate the sentiment any the more for that.

'There's no need to scowl.' He laughed. 'If it's any consolation, you look considerably less lost and abandoned now. You just look permanently angry.'

She wished that he wouldn't use that tone of voice with her. That very slightly patronising voice which made her feel as though she was still back in school.

'Only when I'm with you,' she said with disdain, which made him look even more amused. 'When I'm at work I'm perfectly normal, and I'm not at all angry with Robert.'

'Robert?' He frowned and tried to sort through his

memory bank to come up with a face that might fit the
name.

'He works with me,' she clarified, thinking of the
good-natured face and the red hair.

'And you get along well with him, do you?'

She smiled. 'Like a house on fire. He's very sweet
tempered and great fun.'

'Should I be warned of the start of boyfriends pounding at the front door so that they can get in to see you?'

'There's no need to be sarcastic,' Suzanne said, irritated. She had never had a line of boyfriends trying to
break down the front door so that they could get in to
see her, and he knew that. She just wasn't the type that
attracted flocks of men and she never had been. There
was nothing provocative about her. She never swayed
on high heels, or wore tight clothes, or did elaborate
things to her hair. He must have known that very well.

'Anyway,' she added, 'Robert has a girlfriend.'

'Oh, dear. Was that a great disappointment for you?'

'If I was desperate for a boyfriend, which I assure you
I'm not, then I would go out and find one,' Suzanne
snapped. She made that sound as though finding a com-
patible male was just a question of supermarket shopping. 'Would you like that? Would it set your mind at
rest? You wouldn't have to fear that I might start getting
ideas above my station.'

'Now,' he drawled, giving her the full blast of that
dry charm of his, 'is there any reason for me to fear
that?'

'None at all.'

'What a relief. Does that mean that I needn't lock my
bedroom door at night?'

Suzanne tried not to let her teeth snap together. She
tried to hold onto an even temper. She even tried to
smile, although she was afraid that what emerged bore

closer resemblance to a kind of demented baring of the teeth.

'That's right.'

'And I take it that you're not afraid of my breaking down your bedroom door?'

Very amusing, she wanted to say. You were tired, and how well I've done my job in cheering you up by providing some light comic relief.

'That's right.'

'Why are you so sure?'

'Because,' she said tightly, 'as we've already established, I'm not your cup of tea any more than you are mine.' She stood up because that was the only way she felt that the conversation could be brought to an end. If she kept sitting where she was, half hanging off the edge of the chair with her fingernails grimly biting into the cushion, then he would simply continue baiting her until the cows came home, because it was entertaining him.

'Not going already?' he asked, standing up and walking towards her with a half-grin on his face. 'And you were doing such a good job of getting rid of my weariness.'

'So I noticed,' she said coldly. 'When feeling stressed, just take two spoonfuls of my infantile company and you'll have a good night's sleep.'

'Don't be foolish.' The grin vanished from his face and he was looking at her seriously, which was almost as bad because her nerves began to jump. 'When you're not feeling sorry for yourself, you're very light-hearted. Your naïvety is refreshing.'

But never stimulating, she thought. For a man like him, stimulating came in small, sexy packages like Angela Street, whom she found as hard as ice but who was probably very compliant when it came to her lover. She was the sort of woman who would attract him. No refreshing naïvety there, that was for sure. Just hard intel-

ligence and the sort of looks that turned heads. Whatever
he said, how could she not believe that there was more
to that relationship than he was telling?

'You should thank your upbringing for that,' he was
saying, standing right in front of her, so that she could
almost breathe in his masculinity. 'Your father did a
good job, Suzie.'

The breath caught in her throat, and she looked down,
away from that disturbing, aggressive face. 'I know
that,' she said. 'I never missed not having a mother. He
was more than enough, and I can't believe that he's gone
out of my life for ever. There was so much I had left to
say to him.'

One hot tear trickled down her face. She hated being
vulnerable and exposed like this in front of him, but she
couldn't resist the need to talk.

'I know,' Dane said gently. 'But he's not gone, you
know. You have a lifetime's worth of memories.'

The single tear was joined by another one, and she
muttered unsteadily, 'I'm very sorry.'

'What for?' his voice was surprised, but even so she
hurriedly wiped her face with her arm and sniffed.

'For being so maudlin.'

He didn't say anything. He reached out and put both
his arms around her and pulled her towards him in an
embrace that seemed to enfold every part of her. Her
cheek pressed against his chest. She could hear the
steady beating of his heart underneath the shirt. His
hands stroked her hair—a soothing gesture—and he
murmured, 'Shh,' as though she had said something, although she hadn't.

She laughed nervously and pulled back, looking up at
him. Some flippant remark would have been just the
thing right now, because suddenly the atmosphere had
thickened, and even if that was just in her imagination
it still made her feel jumpy and unsettled.

'Silly Suzie,' was the only thing she could think of saying, and a ghost of a smile lightened his face.

The arms which had been around her were now less tight, and she could feel his palms splayed out against her back. His thumb was on her ribcage. Could he feel her rapidly beating heart?

'Stop crying yourself down,' he said softly, and she gave him a watery smile. Her mouth, she thought idiotically, was only inches away from his own. He had a very nice mouth—firm but sensual at the same time. She could imagine what it might feel to have it cover hers, and the thought made her feel hot and agitated.

His hands shifted slightly, under her breasts. He inclined his head, down, towards her, and kissed her on the forehead, which wasn't alarming at all, was it? The local vicar had done exactly the same thing at the funeral. She tried to replace the lean, hard-boned man against her with the safe, plump image of the vicar, and for a while she succeeded. For about two seconds, then her senses went haywire again and all she could think was that she was being held by Dane Sutherland. Even if it was a thoroughly comforting caress.

'Feeling better?' he asked and his voice came to her as from miles away.

'Yes. Thank you. Much better.' She could hardly get the words out. Her mouth felt as though it was stuffed with cotton wool. She shifted a bit, but he didn't remove his arms. Did he think that she might fall down without his support? In point of fact, her legs did feel a bit on the wobbly side and she put that down to the unexpected onslaught of unhappiness that had overtaken her a short while ago. Emotional upsets tended to make you feel weak and unstable. She was quite sure that that was a documented medical fact.

'Good.' He paused. 'Whatever you may think of me, however much you may dislike and blame me for what happened to your father, and,' he couldn't help adding, 'however ridiculous and unfounded your accusations may be, it's far better for you to release your emotions than bottle them up inside you.' Their eyes met and she blinked. What was he telling her? That he was willing to fit the bill of the handy shoulder to cry on?

It occurred to her that she would have liked rather more than that and she quickly shoved the thought aside.

'Yes, you're right,' she agreed, and gave him a watery smile.

He didn't propose to have a long conversation with her in this position, did he? She hoped not, because every nerve in her body was agonisingly aware of him.

'You mean you agree with me?' He gave a low, sexy laugh under his breath. 'I must put that in my diary.'

He kissed her again on her forehead, and then, while her face was still tilted up to his, he bent lower and kissed her on her mouth—a light, undemanding kiss.

Anyone with an ounce of sympathy for a girl in distress would have kissed in a similar manner. She attempted to pin down the image of the vicar again and failed utterly. She couldn't visualise the vicar kissing anyone on the mouth, not even his wife, and she certainly couldn't visualise anyone responding to an innocent kiss from him with such shameful longing—not even his wife.

He kissed her again on her mouth, but this time his lips stayed on hers.

Suzanne felt her body tremble in his arms and his kiss deepened. With a gasp of shock she felt the pressure of his mouth on hers increase and the feel of his tongue in her mouth sent waves of forbidden pleasure rushing through her. Her fingers tightened on the collar of his shirt, and her breasts, pressed against his chest, were aching with desire.

His hands moved slightly. She wished that he would

move them up and over her breasts; she wished that he would ease the hardened nipples, caress them. She closed her eyes and shuddered, torn between knowing that this was all wrong, however wonderful it might feel, and a craving to let him continue.

The choice was taken out of her hands, because he stepped back from her and looked at her with darkened eyes. His breathing was as erratic as hers was.

'I think,' he said with a shuttered expression, 'that it's time you went to bed, don't you?'

He turned his back and walked across to the window and stood there, staring out, waiting for her to leave.

Suzanne watched him and couldn't, for the life of her, think of a single thing to say that might rescue the situation. She had never felt so humiliated in her entire existence.

She remained where she was for a few seconds, hesitant, and then left the room quietly and slowly. She wasn't going to run. She walked with carefully measured steps out of the room and along to her bedroom, and once she was inside she shut the door, quietly and carefully as well.

But she didn't switch on the light. Instead she went across to her bed and sat on it and replayed with deliberate slowness what had happened a few moments ago.

The most consoling thought was that maybe he would blame himself, maybe he would think that he had taken advantage of a poor, innocent young girl who had been in a state of stress.

Unfortunately he would, she acknowledged miserably to herself, have to be a certified idiot not to have realised that her response to him had been anything but unwilling.

She hadn't tried to stop him, had she? She had clung—clung and returned his kiss because even if her mind had told her not to her body had gone beyond listening to what her mind had to say.

He wasn't attracted to her, and she groaned when she thought how eagerly she had pressed herself against him.

What must he have been thinking when he had been holding her substantial frame?

She got undressed in darkness, not really relishing the thought of seeing naked proof of her unfashionable curves. She very nearly, in fact, felt the urge to have a little taste of chocolate, but it was a passing thought. She had lost the taste for it as quickly as she had found it. Indeed, she hadn't had any chocolate for a while, ever since he had stormed into her life and filled it with something other than her continuous, never-ending misery.

Without trying, she had lost weight. Never enough to reduce her to Angela's size, she knew. For that she would have needed to lop a few inches off here, there and just about everywhere, but her clothes no longer sat snugly on her, and a couple of things had been relegated to the back of the cupboard. She would have to do some alterations on them in time. She would have to learn how to manipulate a needle and thread—another ladylike trait which she had never been able to grasp with any degree of proficiency.

Suzanne stayed in bed longer than usual the following morning, giving Dane plenty of time to leave the house, and when she decided that the coast was clear she finally emerged.

She didn't want to bump into him. She didn't want to have to witness that glinting smile on his lips as his thoughts flew back to that brief lapse on his part. Nor did she wish to hear any tedious remarks along the lines of 'My, but I hadn't realised what a big girl you had become'.

She hesitantly entered the kitchen and, of course, there

he was sitting at the kitchen table with a coffee-cup in his hand, in front of the *Financial Times*, and her heart plummeted to somewhere close to her ankles.

'Hi.' She turned her back on him and began fixing herself a piece of toast and some tea.

He was dressed for work, apart from the jacket which was draped over the back of one of the chairs. He clearly had a cavalier attitude towards his clothes, but then, she thought, he had enough money to indulge that kind of attitude. If his suits collapsed, then he could afford to replace them instantly and not have to root through a DIY manual on darning and mending.

'I've been waiting for you,' he said in a closed voice, and she could feel his eyes on her back, which made her fumble a bit with the butter.

'Oh?' She finally had no option but to face him, which she did, though virtually behind her cup of tea and her piece of toast. 'I'm sorry,' she lied. 'I would have come out sooner if I'd known that. I was enjoying having a lie in.' Another lie. She had been up for hours, thinking and mentally kicking herself.

'I want to apologise for last night,' he said without a trace of embarrassment, but then, of course, he was a sophisticated man of the world and she was a country bumpkin.

'Oh, that's quite all right,' Suzanne said, dying of mortification. 'No harm done. I guess we were both not ourselves.' This seemed as good an excuse to stick to as any. 'I was terribly upset for some reason. I thought that I was beginning to come to terms with Dad's death, but suddenly it was as if I was back there in time, and I know you were tired. It was late. It just happened. Not—' she laughed as though she were quite accustomed to dealing with awkward situations like this '—that anything happened at all!'

He looked at her in silence for such a long time that

she began to replay what she had said in her head, wondering if she had made some horrendous gaffe somewhere along the line.

'Fine.' His voice was even cooler than it had been to start with, which she resented. Hadn't she just saved him an apology by launching herself into an elaborate one of her own, for God's sake?

He stood up and said to her, without blinking, 'One little lesson, though, Suzie. We go back a long way so we can both jot this down to unfortunate experience, but don't think that another man might not think that you're leading him on. That really is the way that unfortunate experiences happen.' He slipped on his jacket while she was still staring at him, open-mouthed and red-faced.

'I can take care of myself, thank you,' she said tightly. 'Guardian angel isn't one of your duties to me!'

She had more to say on the subject, but he already had his back to her, and before she could mutter another word he had walked out, leaving her with the feeling that somehow the blame for what had happened had landed squarely on her shoulders.

CHAPTER FIVE

For the next few weeks Suzanne made a determined effort to keep out of Dane's way. She also started looking for somewhere else to live, but that was turning out to be a nightmare. Now that she was in the position of not having to find somewhere, she discovered that she could look at the various bedsits with a critical eye, and what she saw did not appeal. Rent in London was steep and for what she could afford she could just about manage another bedsit, slightly higher up the scale than the last one that she had occupied, but still cramped, forlorn and unappealing.

After her fifth abortive trek to somewhere desolate in Acton, she returned to the apartment to find him, for once, home before her and sitting in the lounge with his briefcase in front of him, a laptop computer on the table and papers spread everywhere.

'My goodness,' she said, stepping in between the paperwork and trying not to eye him but very conscious of his eyes on her, 'it looks as though a hurricane passed through here.'

'Where have you been?' He had been pouring over documents with a red pen, writing things in the margins, but now he sat back on the sofa and looked at her with his hands behind his head.

Suzanne wasn't looking at him. She was looking at the chair and wondering how she could reach it without stepping on one of the bits of paper.

'You'll never make it,' he informed her drily. 'Stay where you are. We're going out for something to eat.'

'We are?' She glanced at him, disconcerted, and he began gathering up the paper, stopping to read bits along the way.

'We are,' he said in a distracted voice. 'I take it you haven't eaten as yet?'

'No, but—'

'That's settled then.' He stood up, flexed his muscles and looked at her with amusement. She had been standing on one foot, preparing to hop nimbly across the room to the sanctuary of the chair on the other side. 'You look like a stork,' he said, smiling that perfectly enchanting smile of his which could make her heart flip over even when she had spent hours steeling herself not to react.

'Your average stork might be irritated at that comparison,' she said, and he laughed and stuck his hands in his pockets.

They hadn't indulged in this sort of light-hearted banter for a while. In fact, she had hardly seen him at all recently. He usually left for work long before her and returned long after she had come back.

She was also feeling rather light-hearted, despite the useless trek halfway across London to view a bedsit that had looked as though it had stepped straight out of the Victorian era. It had been a brilliant day, and even though it was now after seven-thirty it was still warm and sunny.

'I'm hardly dressed for the occasion,' she said, glancing down at her jeans and striped shirt which she had rolled up to the elbows.

'Oh, you look all right to me,' he drawled, and she immediately wished that she hadn't drawn attention to herself, because he was staring at her now, in the sort of thorough way that made her feel silly and confused.

'Besides,' he continued, and his eyes returned to her face, 'you have no idea where I'm taking you.'

'True. Fast-food joints don't have a dress code, do they?' She spun around on her heels and made for the door. 'Just as well since they're the only places I can afford to eat and my usual dress code wouldn't pass muster at most normal establishments.'

She had half expected him to return an ironic murmur of agreement, but he was silent behind her and she had to resist the temptation to glance around and try and read the expression on his face.

'Not a fast-food joint,' he said, and he was closer to her than she had realised, because she could feel his warm breath on the back of her neck. 'Just a quick Italian.'

'Let me take you somewhere,' she said impulsively, spinning round to face him.

'You just said that you could only afford to eat at burger joints.'

'And wouldn't you like to share the experience?' She hardly thought that he would agree. She doubted that he had ever been into a burger joint in his life, or if he had then it had been years ago and probably just in passing. Extravagantly wealthy businessmen didn't make burger bars their first port of call usually.

'If you like,' he said with a crooked smile, as though he could read her mind, and she grinned back at him.

'I like,' she murmured. 'Although—' she gave him the critical, assessing look he specialised in '—I'm not sure your dress code is quite right for what I have in mind.'

But he didn't change, as she'd known he wouldn't, and they found themselves, less than forty minutes later and after a hasty trip along the underground, sitting in a crowded, fluorescent lit, burger joint, in front of two trays and several containers of the mandatory burgers, chips and colas.

Because of the fine weather the pavements were still teeming with people, lots of them tourists, and a lot more appeared to have teemed into the fast-food restaurant.

Suzanne lowered her eyes and tried not to smile at the sexy man sitting opposite her, in his work trousers and expensive white shirt.

'I don't suppose you come to places like this very often,' she said in a demure voice, and he raised one eyebrow.

'I don't suppose I want to,' he returned. 'Although...' his grey eyes strayed to the queues at the cash tills, behind which dozens of people where hurrying about packing boxes of burgers and filling cups with soft drinks '...it certainly seems to be popular.' He held up his burger and eyed it sceptically. 'I do wonder whether this can actually be classified as belonging to the food chain, though.'

Suzanne laughed, amused. 'What a condescending thing to say,' she told him gravely, digging into her meal with relish. She hadn't eaten a burger for a long time and it tasted good, whatever he had to say on the subject.

'So you never answered my question,' he said to her, halfway through the meal. He had discarded the plastic top of the cup and was drinking his cola without the straw.

'What question?'

'Where did you go after work?'

'Oh.' She shrugged and picked up a couple of chips, which were quite cold now but nice anyway. 'I was out flat-hunting.'

'Flat-hunting?' He frowned. 'What for?'

'For a flat, of course,' she said patiently, and his frown deepened.

'I've already made it clear to you that you needn't leave my place.'

'I thought you would be pleased,' she said, refusing to be alarmed by the dark expression on his face.

'Why the hell should I be pleased at the prospect of having to trudge across London to rescue you from another disgusting tip posing as a flat?'

'As I've kept telling you, there was no need to trudge across London to rescue me in the first place. Why did you, anyway?'

'Because,' he said slowly, 'after a few passing-through visits I was back in England to stay, and I suppose you were a link with the past—the only link I felt inclined to seek out.'

'Martha being out of the question.'

'That's right.'

'For reasons which you won't explain.'

'Not at this moment in time, at any rate.' He gave her a half-smile in acknowledgement of her tenacity, then continued, 'Suffice it to say that I always remembered you with great affection, and I was worried when I learned that you had vanished into London after your father died. Hence my appearance on your doorstep. Which brings me to my original point. I don't relish another rescue mission to another disgusting tip.'

'I wouldn't rent a tip,' she told him, sulky because she hated it when he treated her like a child that needed looking after instead of a woman who was quite capable of looking after herself. *Always remembered her with affection?* He made her sound like a pet dog.

'You made the mistake once before,' he pointed out.

'I can afford to be more choosy now,' Suzanne said. 'I'm not desperate and homeless, and I'm earning far more now than I was when I first came to London.' It seemed like years since she had first arrived, forcing herself to be optimistic when misery was always there, knocking on the door.

'And what have you managed to find?' he asked, in a cool sort of voice that forestalled a glowing report.

'Nothing very much,' she admitted. 'It's very difficult.' She looked at him accusingly. 'I've been spoilt living in your apartment. Nothing compares to it. At least, nothing that falls within my range.'

'Then why are you bothering to look?'

'Because I can't stay with you for ever!' She frowned, not looking at him. 'I know you might be banking on the fact that the country girl will inevitably go back to where she belongs, but you might end up waiting longer than you bargained for and I can't stay with you in the meanwhile.'

The chips looked absolutely disgusting now, as did the remainder of her beefburger, which had gone cold as well, and she shoved both aside and linked her fingers together on the table in front of her.

'It's time I moved on,' she said seriously, although the thought of moving on filled her with a kind of numbness which she didn't want to stop and analyse. 'I mean—' she glanced up at him '—you can't tell me that my presence doesn't put you off...off...you know what...'

'What are you talking about now, for heaven's sake?'

'Bringing women back.' For women, she thought, read Angela Street. 'I haven't seen any at all at the apartment since I arrived, though I'm sure there must have been some before I came on the scene.' Her words tripped over one another, and she found that she couldn't quite meet his eyes.

'You make me sound like a rampant animal,' he replied mildly, but with a thread of amusement in his voice that irritated her.

'Just a normal man with normal...normal...you know.' Her face was red.

'Urges?' he supplied helpfully, and that made her go redder. 'And what do you know about a man's urges, Suzie?'

'Stop laughing at me,' she snapped, glaring at him, and he tried to look suitably chastised, which made her glare harder.

'I was not laughing at you,' he said with a grin. Then his face sobered and he leant forward and said softly, 'Not at all.'

His voice was like a caress, but before she could analyse that he had stood up, terminating the conversation, and she followed suit. They didn't head back to the apartment, though. They strolled around Leicester Square, which was almost glorious in the mellow evening light. It was only when they were in the taxi, driving back to the apartment, that she said lightly, 'Anyway, you're stuck with me for the time being because the places I've looked at have been awful.' She sighed and stared out of the window. 'How easy it is to become accustomed to the good life.' It was only recently that she had really understood how difficult it would have been for her father to have left the grounds of the Sutherlands' mansion. How could a cold, bleak terraced house in the town centre have compared to the idyllic, rose-clad cottage surrounded by the sprawling lawns?

'Isn't it ironic,' she said, turning to look at him and seeing only the highlights of his face in the darkened car, 'how I am now dependent on you for somewhere to live, just as Dad was on your father? I even work for you!'

'The irony is only in your eyes.'

'I don't think so.'

'And do you imagine that your fate at my hands will

duplicate your father's fate at the hands of my step-mother?'

'I have no idea,' Suzanne replied uncomfortably, aware that their conversation had drifted into uneasy waters, though there had been no way of preventing that.

'Are you telling me that you equate me with Martha?' The inflection in his voice when he mentioned his step-mother was odd, drained of expression, and she shook her head.

'Then there's no problem, is there?' His eyes glittered like hard jewels in his face.

'No.' She wouldn't repeat what Angela had said to her—the frequent, carefully clothed reminders that she must surely be starting to long for a place of her own, somewhere where she could stretch her wings.

Angela always gave the impression that she and Dane shared the same views. Did they? Suzanne was beginning to doubt it. She was beginning to doubt that they discussed anything but work. What she couldn't doubt, though, was that Angela intended to have him and that she was as single-minded as she was beautiful—a lethal combination for any man in the firing line.

The taxi pulled up in front of the block of apartments and she heard the driver give a low whistle under his breath. Security lights gave the building a dramatic orange glow so that it seemed almost ethereal. Was it any wonder, she thought, that everything she had seen so far had lacked a certain something?

She looked at Dane surreptitiously as they walked towards the building and the parallel between her situation and her father's sprang to mind once more. Except, and something stirred darkly inside her, her dependence was more complicated. If the plug was pulled and she found herself without a house and without a job, she would also be without him in her life, and she realised that that disturbed her far more than she wanted to think. She looked away quickly, her heart beating like a drum, and she found that she couldn't look at him as they entered the apartment.

'Are you going to carry on working?' she asked politely, hovering by the kitchen door, and he nodded. 'Don't you ever stop working?'

'I thought that I just had.' He ran himself some water from the tap and took a long mouthful of it before depositing the empty glass into the sink.

He walked towards her and she felt the heat begin to course through her body.

'Well,' she said, 'thank you for an enjoyable evening.' He was standing in front of her and he looked at her with a smile.

'Shouldn't I be thanking you?' he said wryly. 'After all, the meal was your treat. I hope I didn't make too much of a spectacle of myself.'

'What do you mean?' Her cheeks reddened and it was an effort to keep her voice nice and steady.

'You thought that I might be awkward and uncomfortable in a fast-food place, didn't you?'

'No, I didn't!'

'Of course you did. You're so transparent, Suzie. Actually—and don't die of shock on the spot—I have eaten in burger joints before. They litter the streets in America.'

'But they're not your line, are they? You prefer chic, expensive French restaurants with lots of atmosphere and waiters in attendance.'

'Don't.'

'Don't what?'

'Speculate. You're usually wrong.' He laughed but his eyes remained on her face and she was the first to look away. She realised with horror that she didn't want their evening to end here, at the door of the kitchen. She wanted it to end in a bedroom, on a bed, and she clenched her fists in anger at such an unwanted desire.

'I'll try and stop the habit,' she replied, keeping her voice light. 'But, right now, no more thoughts for me. I'm off to bed.'

She turned to walk away and he said to her lazily, 'Oh, by the way, I forgot to mention this but there's a party here on Saturday evening.'

'And you'd like me to go out?' was the first thing that sprang to mind.

'Don't be utterly stupid,' he grated, unsmiling. 'You're invited. There'll be about forty people.'

'Is it to do with work?' she asked, and he shook his head.

'Quite a few people from America,' he said. 'The rest are friends and colleagues of mine from London.'

Would he have asked her if he had had a choice? She couldn't envisage him sending out a gilded invitation to the daughter of his father's chauffeur to meet his friends and colleagues, but she didn't voice her thoughts.

'And what will everyone be wearing?'

'I have no idea.' He shrugged as though he didn't really give a damn, but then he would look good in anything. It was different for her, though. She didn't want to turn up dressed in a suit, to find everyone else in jeans and a shirt, nor did she want to come in informal wear and be mistaken for a bag lady who had lost her way.

'Should I wear a dress?' she asked bluntly, and he looked at her.

'Do you possess any?'

There was an implied insult there somewhere, she felt sure, and her hackles rose.

'I could buy one,' she said coldly. 'As a matter of fact, I've been thinking of investing in one lately.' She hadn't really. She was quite happy to carry on as she was, in her jeans and jumpers garb, but now that she had voiced the thought it occurred to her that brightening up her image might not be a bad idea at all.

'Why not? It might be interesting to discover whether you have legs under those jeans you're wearing every time I see you.' He raised one eyebrow and grinned but she wasn't in the mood for grinning back. 'Oh, dear,' he said with heavy pretence of woe. 'Was that a misdirected remark?'

He was laughing as she flounced off to her bedroom and she didn't lay eyes on him the following morning because he had already gone by the time she dragged herself out of the house, only coming alive once she had reached her office and gulped down a cup of coffee.

Robert was intrigued at the thought of a party at the big boss's house.

'How come I wasn't invited?' he asked. 'What's wrong with me?' He sniffed under his arms and grinned at her from across his desk. 'Would you tell me if I had a body-odour problem?'

Suzanne returned his grin and said, 'Of course I wouldn't. I would just ask for your desk to be moved to another part of the building. Anyway, the only reason I shall be going along is because he has no choice, short of asking me to vacate the premises between the hours of eight and one, and he wouldn't do that.'

'Wouldn't he?' He appeared to give this some thought. 'He could teach my girlfriend a thing or two in that case. She's always asking me to do that.' Which made Suzanne laugh.

She found over the next day that she was actually planning quite seriously what she would wear to Dane's wretched party. She had never been to a party where casual wear hadn't been the dress code. What did people wear to more formal things? What was the dividing line between nicely sophisticated and brassily dressed to kill?

Angela would know. She seemed to know everything there was to know about clothes, but Suzanne had no intention of asking for advice. The more she saw of the other woman, the less she liked her, and apart from necessity she made sure that their paths did not cross.

She spent the Friday lunchtime shopping—a pastime she so irregularly indulged in that it took her twice as long to find anything because she didn't know where to begin. Big stores confused her and small boutiques she found threatening. The sales assistants all looked like models and she had to resist the temptation to find a convenient rack of clothes and hide behind it.

So it was after one by the time she returned to her desk, flatly refusing to let Robert have a look at her purchases.

'Anything sexy?' he asked in a suggestive tone of voice, which was like water off a duck's back to her, and she replied absent-mindedly, not looking at him, already involved in columns of figures and reports on company accounts for a firm they were hoping to acquire.

'Hardly. I'm not exactly Brigitte Bardot, am I?'

'You might be if you stopped wearing unflattering suits all the time.'

'And wore what instead?' She glanced up at him, disconcerted that he found her clothes unflattering. As far as she was concerned, there was nothing wrong with them. Some were a bit loose now because she had lost quite a bit of weight, but on the whole they did their job. 'Mini skirts and boots?'

Robert ran his fingers through his bright hair, which made it stick up in various directions. 'Yes, that might work.'

'Not for me. I'm not that type.'

'You've never tried.'

'Nor do I feel tempted to.'

'You can be very boring at times,' he told her, which produced an involuntary smile on her lips.

'What a joy you are.'

The sight of Angela standing at the doorway, looking at them, reduced them to immediate silence. She was dressed in a striking black suit and as she stood there Suzanne thought uncharitably that she resembled some kind of venomous insect. Beautiful and deadly, probably belonging to a species that ate its young.

'I see you two are hard at work,' she drawled.

'Yes, we are,' Suzanne said seriously, her eyes wide and innocent. 'Actually, I was just putting the finishing touches to my report on Algiban. I shall have them typed and ready for you by the end of the afternoon.'

'Good.' Angela paused. 'And those accounts I asked you to have a look at?'

'Done.' Suzanne gave her an efficient, helpful smile and Robert was trying to suppress his mirth.

'You're ahead of schedule.' The perfect mouth cracked into a smile of sorts.

'Yes, I am,' Suzanne agreed, smiling back, 'although I'm just working at my own pace.' She was, she knew, a quick and thorough worker. She enjoyed ferreting out bits of information and putting the pieces together. She found it fascinating. She hadn't for a long time, but working here had revitalized an interest in figures and deductions and company accounts which she had believed to be dead and buried.

'That's good. I'm just on my way to a meeting with Bill Cooper from Sales, but if you could spare a few moments, Suzanne...?'

Suzanne stood up and wondered why she'd bothered to phrase the command as a question. She saw out of the corner of her eye that Robert was busy shuffling papers and lighting a cigarette. He had cut down his intake to five a day but he always made sure that he lit one whenever Angela walked in because he knew that it irritated her. On cue, she was wrinkling her nose and looking at the cigarette with distaste.

She strode off in the direction of her office and Suzanne followed, clutching her reports, comfortable in the knowledge that there was no question that she couldn't answer.

But reports were not, she discovered as soon as she had sat down, to be the object of the exercise. Angela gave them a cursory glance and then said, out of the blue, 'Dane tells me that you've been invited to the little bash tomorrow night.'

'Yes, I have,' Suzanne replied obediently. She had learnt fast that volunteering information was a wasted exercise. Any attempts at friendliness had met with a stone wall of tight-lipped non-communication. Angela didn't like her. She had been forced to employ her but she had no intention of being amicable about it, and since the feeling was mutual Suzanne was quite happy to endure the stony looks. The job was the consolation. It was well paid and invigorating and more than made up for the hostility.

'There's absolutely no need for you to attend,' Angela said, trying to sound kindly but not succeeding very well. 'I expect you'll find the whole thing very boring.'

'It might be fun,' Suzanne told her perversely.

'You'll be far and away the youngest person there,' Angela informed her. She linked her fingers together on the desk and sat forward, which made Suzanne feel as though she was attending an interview. Did that observation require an answer of sorts? she wondered. She smiled and didn't say anything.

'I'm sure you'd be happier going out with your friends. You've made a few since you arrived in London, I take it?'

'Yes, quite a few.' She had become quite friendly, in

fact, with several of the girls from the company. She had also renewed contact with her old friends. They had acted as though there had been no time lapse at all, for which Suzanne had been instantly and immensely grateful.

'It would be churlish of me to turn down Dane's invitation, though,' she added, knowing that this was the very last thing Angela would want to hear, and she could tell from the tightening of the lips that she had struck bull's eye. But what could the other woman say to that?

'Of course it would be. And I'm sure that Dane would be quite disappointed if his favourite little protégé wasn't there. We thought, though, that you might enjoy helping out with the serving of the drinks. The caterers will be doing the food, and there will be a waiter, of course, but I'm sure you'd rather help him instead of having to mingle with fuddy-duddies reliving old times.'

This had been a joint idea? She doubted that, but as always with everything Angela implied there was still that tenacious shade of uncertainty tugging away at the back of her mind, undermining all her logical reasons for disbelieving everything the other woman said.

'Of course,' Angela continued hurriedly, 'it's up to you, but at least if you're being useful you might be able to wriggle out of the dull small talk.' She gave a high, tinkling laugh. 'I can remember when I was your age my parents' parties always seemed so tedious.'

'Did they entertain a lot?' Suzanne asked, biting back some caustic retorts, and Angela's eyes slid away from hers.

'Quite a bit, yes,' she said, standing up. 'Not that you would be interested in hearing about my parents.' She moved towards the door and said briskly, 'Now, I do hope you won't run back to Dane and mention any of our little conversation?'

'Why should I?' Suzanne smiled sweetly. 'I'm awfully grateful to him for doing what he's done, but I know my place.'

'You're a sensible thing,' Angela said, and even in high heels she still had to look up at Suzanne as she said this. 'It's reflected in your work. You're very switched on. Now, I must dash. If John Grieves calls, could you take the message? It's important. I'm hoping to net him as a very big customer indeed.'

'Of course. And I'll see you tomorrow.' She could hardly get the words out because she felt so bitter and angry.

How dared Angela imply that she would be better off serving drinks? she raged to herself that evening. And even if Dane hadn't said a word of the sort, was that what he thought too?

She knew what she was going to do now, though. It had come to her in a resentful, blinding flash as she'd taken the tube home after work, and she headed off on Saturday morning, walking quickly, head down, fists clenched. To the shops.

There was certainly no need for her to be around during the day. The place was full of caterers, who were preparing vast quantities of food. It was to be a cold buffet but with very fancy salads, cold meats and various varieties of bread, and then lots of puddings.

The kitchen counter, when she returned later in the afternoon, was groaning under the weight of food. Suzanne drifted past it and was instantly given a guided tour of each dish by the chef, who was a dark-haired, effeminate man with an appealing manner.

'Normally,' he whispered to her confidentially, 'I would be able to leave the running of the show to my assistant, but Derek—naughty boy—has gone on holiday, and this one—' he flicked his dark eyes in the direction of a gangling youth who was earnestly putting the finishing touches to the sherry trifle '—can't be relied upon. I've seen the way he did some of the carrot roses to decorate the smoked salmon. Most unprofessional.'

His finishing touches to the trifle seemed highly professional from where she was standing, but who was she to voice an opinion on the subject? She was only just coming to terms with the simplest of dishes.

'Well,' she said, after having admired everything, as tact dictated, to excess, 'I shall see you later, no doubt. I shall be helping behind the scenes. Serving drinks, actually.'

'But... You don't live here?'

'I do. Temporarily. I'm a lodger. I think it might be fun to play the waitress, though. Get away from ageing businessmen and polite chit-chat.'

And she left the chef standing with a look of complete bemusement on his face.

Later she heard Dane's voice, talking in that authoritative manner, then some low laughter, and later still, just before the guests were due to arrive, he knocked on her door and asked her whether she intended to emerge from her bedroom at all that evening, to which she said, through the closed door, that she was just about to get dressed.

She hadn't even stepped into the bath as yet, in point of fact. She intended taking her time and making her grand entrance once the guests had all arrived.

At eight, she stepped into the bath, where she soaked for as long as she possibly could without emerging looking like a wrinkled prune. Then she carefully brushed her hair. She had had it trimmed since she'd begun working for Angela, though it hadn't been noticeable, since she always wore her hair tied back. It would never be straight, but it rippled quite attractively now that it had been rescued from her lack of attention.

Then she applied her make-up. This was trickier. She

normally didn't use a great deal of it, so she took her time. Not too much, she decided. No eye-shadow at all, just mascara. Some blusher. Some lipstick, but not bright red. She didn't feel comfortable with bright red lipstick. If she had had the time, she would have done her nails as well, but she had left it too late. She could hear the low hum of conversation drifting along the corridor to her bedroom, which meant that the guests had probably all arrived.

She finished dressing quickly. She didn't want Dane striding to her bedroom and impatiently hauling her out. That would spoil everything.

When everything was in place, she stood back and looked at herself in the mirror, and the first thing that crossed her mind was that she had lost a great deal of weight over the weeks. She wasn't skinny—she never would be—but she could actually see a waist now and her stomach was flat once again. Her legs looked pretty good too. She had always had good legs—long with slender ankles—and right now there was a good deal of them to be seen. Well, Dane had sarcastically remarked that he never saw her legs, hadn't he? He was about to get an eyeful of them now.

She grinned and walked out of her bedroom.

CHAPTER SIX

EVERYONE had arrived. The apartment was big, but forty-odd people filled it out at the seams, and there was the steady, high noise of voices trying to rise above each other. Two waiters were manfully doing the rounds with trays.

Suzanne's gaze roved across the room and met Dane's eyes just as he caught sight of her. He had been talking to a group of four people but he'd looked straight across the room almost as soon as she'd walked in. As had nearly everyone else, including the group around him. There was a brief lull in the conversation—time enough for her to absorb the effect that she had had in her small black waitress's outfit, with the tiny white frilly apron in front, and the black high heels which put her on eye-level with most of the men there.

She couldn't remember ever having had this effect on a roomful of people before. The initial heady effect began to wear off and she smiled weakly at the sea of faces staring at her. Should she say hello? She was spared the decision because Dane announced, without a trace of humour in his voice, 'While all your attention is riveted on the girl by the doorway, I might as well take this opportunity to introduce her to you. Suzanne Stanton is an old friend of the family and is staying with me temporarily.'

There were some appreciative murmurs, the conver-

sation resumed and she hesitantly approached Dane and
his group of friends.

The high heels felt uncomfortable. She wasn't accustomed to wearing anything but flat shoes, and she had
to move slowly, even though she was aware that that
gave her a certain swaying walk. She could feel eyes
following her progress across the room and she tried to
be oblivious to them.

She finally, after what seemed like hours of weaving
through the crowd, managed to make it to Dane's side
and she politely listened while he made introductions.

'When I mentioned that it was to be informal,' he said
in a hard voice, 'I had no idea that you would take me
so literally.'

She met his eyes and realised that he wasn't in the
least amused at her get-up. He was mad, coldly angry,
his grey eyes cool and shuttered, his mouth a narrow
line.

Angela, standing next to him, didn't look particularly
impressed either, but Suzanne didn't care about that. She
smiled brightly and said to no one in particular, 'It was
suggested that I might like to help out with serving
drinks, so I thought that I'd dress for the occasion.' It
had seemed like a good idea at the time, but she was
rapidly beginning to revise her thoughts on the matter.

'I'm glad that you did,' one of the men said to her,
and she looked at him with a gush of relief. He was
young, American, with sandy-coloured hair and blue
eyes. He was smiling at her, his arms folded with a half-
empty drink in one hand.

She looked at him and said brightly, indicating his
drink, 'I might as well get the ball rolling with you.'

She reached out to take his glass and Dane said in a
voice that could cut through steel, 'There are waiters
hired to serve drinks, Suzanne. There is no need for you
to help. If you're happy staying in that ridiculous outfit,

then by all means do so, but I will not have you fetching and carrying.'

There was nothing she could find to say to this and she continued to smile through the uncomfortable silence that followed.

'I personally think you look magnificent,' the young American said, and the woman standing next to him murmured something along similar lines, but Angela clearly didn't agree. Her blue eyes were pale and icy and her red mouth was sucked in. She looked like a tiny statue, perfectly painted but as untouchable as marble.

'Thank you.' Suzanne averted her eyes from both Dane and Angela and looked at the sandy-haired American with a great rush of gratitude. 'You're very kind.'

'Honest,' he amended with a flirtatious smile which did wonderful things for her ego.

'Perhaps...' Angela murmured in a voice that was supposed to be what? Suzanne wondered. Kindly? Sisterly? Compassionate? Could a creature of the night be any of those things? 'Perhaps you should slip into something a little less...' she tittered and raised her face to Dane's '...obvious?'

'Perhaps not,' Suzanne told her, directing her remark to Dane as well, and she hoped that he well and truly got the message, because there was no way that she was going to retreat into her bedroom and return suitably attired in something drab and unthreatening. 'Perhaps I happen to think that it might be rather fun to help out serving drinks.' She took the glass from the American, even though he wasn't finished, and demanded what he was drinking, which made him grin even more broadly.

'I must say, I like your style,' he commented, following her as she walked off towards the kitchen. 'Very forceful. Is this the British way of waitressing?' She had her back to him but she could hear the smile in his voice and she began to relax a little.

'Not as far as I'm aware,' she admitted. 'I was sort of trying to make a point.'

She looked at him and he nodded. 'I gather.' Which seemed to make him an ally of sorts for the rest of the evening, and he duly followed her around while she helped to serve the drinks and kept as far away from Dane as space would allow.

After a couple of hours she found that she was actually rather enjoying herself, although that had relatively little to do with the fact that she was waitressing and more to do with the fact that she was the centre of attention wherever she went.

The unattached males tried their best to attach themselves and the attached ones made chivalrous remarks in front of their partners, and all in all she came to the conclusion that she didn't give one damn that out of the corner of her eye she could see Dane watching her, his eyes unsmiling.

The food was excellent. She snatched a plate and actually sat down for half an hour, and discovered with delight that there were quite a few people who seemed to want to sit next to her, and not all of them male.

'It's a pity I'm leaving for New York tomorrow,' her sandy-haired admirer said as he was leaving. His name was Gary Cooper and he had spent some time explaining the insanity of his parents in their choice and the tediousness of people who more or less all said the same thing on being introduced.

'Pity,' Suzanne agreed, smiling, because although she didn't find him sexually attractive she had enjoyed his company.

'If you're ever passing through...?' He gave her his card and she made some light-hearted remark about funds not really catering for fleeting visits to New York.

It was after one o'clock by the time the last guest left. In the mêlée of departing people she had managed to keep her distance from Dane, but now, as she began switching off lights and clearing away the detritus of the party, she was uneasily aware that the click of the door left them both alone in the apartment. And he was still angry. He had made no effort to talk to her during the party, but his silence, she suspected, was not about to continue.

She retreated into the kitchen, where the caterers had left the place almost spotlessly clean, having removed themselves and their equipment with a speed and efficiency that spoke of years of training.

She would have to face him sooner or later and much as she would have preferred the later to the sooner, when at least she would have had some slight advantage in being suitably attired for a confrontation, she guessed that that was wishful thinking.

She began washing the few remaining glasses, with her back to the kitchen door, and she felt him enter without even having to turn round to look. It was true, she thought, when they said that you could feel someone's eyes on you even if you weren't looking in their direction. It was a peculiar feeling—a shivery chill that crept along her spine and made her stiffen in preparation.

'Are you going to face me or are you going to continue washing glasses?'

She turned to face him. He was leaning against the doorway with his hands in the pockets of his olive-green trousers, and his slate-grey eyes were hard—chillingly hard.

'It was a lovely party,' she began in a light voice, her hands occupied with a glass and a teacloth, but she felt awkward in a way that she hadn't earlier on, even though she had been receiving admiring looks from almost every male in the room.

Now, with his eyes on her, she was uncomfortably aware that her skirt was really very short indeed, not reaching anywhere near her knees, and the outline of her breasts was very visible under the skimpy cut of the black top.

'Everything went very well, wouldn't you agree?' she continued bravely. 'The food was delicious. Such a good idea to have a cold buffet. At least there was no problem of people wondering where they could perch themselves so that they could eat. Was there?' He was saying nothing, just looking at her, and she felt some of her bravado beginning to wilt.

'What the hell did you mean by wearing that outfit?' His voice was soft and dangerous and she began to fidget under his unswerving stare.

'I thought that I explained it to you earlier on,' she said, smiling and then almost as quickly wiping the smile from her face because there was no answering one on his.

Silence.

'I know that you wouldn't have asked me if I hadn't been staying under your roof, so I thought that it might be helpful if I did something instead of simply intruding on your get-together.' She wasn't going to try another smile, and she could hear the defensive ring in her voice.

'So you decided to dress for the part.' His mouth twisted but he didn't look away, and that unflinching stare of his was unnerving her more and more. The Spanish inquisitors, she thought, could have learnt a lot from his technique: say little but make sure that the little you say carries a threat implicit in every syllable.

'I thought that it might be fun.'

'Fun to expose most of yourself for the delectation of my guests.'

Put like that, he made it sound cheap and tawdry and she threw him an angry, resentful look from under her lashes.

'You're the only one who didn't seem to like it. Everyone else did.'

'It was a stupid, infantile idea,' he said with scathing distaste, and she flinched.

'Well, what more can you expect from me? I am stupid and infantile. You keep telling me that. I'm sorry if I embarrassed you in front of your friends.'

'Most of the men couldn't take their eyes off you,' he grated under his breath, when he had more or less thought that the topic had been closed. He raked his fingers through his hair and looked at her with frustrated impatience. 'The Cooper boy followed you around the room like a lap-dog for the entire evening.'

So he had noticed. She felt something inside her flicker.

'I liked him. He was nice.'

'He was after one thing.'

'He was not!' she retorted, stung into heated response by the cool dismissiveness in his voice.

'You're very naïve if you think that any man looking at you in that outfit is full of noble thoughts.'

'Not every man has sex on his mind all the time!' Her cheeks were flushed and she could feel herself perspiring lightly. She half turned and deposited the glass and tea-cloth on the kitchen counter, and when she faced him again her arms were wrapped protectively around her.

'But most of them do when they're faced with a body like yours wearing very little.'

It took a few seconds to register, but when it did she couldn't prevent the swift flood of pleasure that filled her. A body like hers. What did he mean? That she was attractive? She remembered his string of girlfriends from the year dot; she remembered Angela too, and the flood of pleasure immediately withered.

'A body like what? I'm too tall, I'm too heavy. I might be naïve and infantile, but I'm not stupid. It never occurred to me that I would become some kind of instant sex object dressed in this get-up.'

He began moving towards her and she pressed herself back against the kitchen counter. Her heart was pounding in her chest and she watched his slow approach with wary fascination.

'Are you blind?'

Her eyes shifted away from his. 'What do you mean?'

'You've lost weight, not that that mattered anyway. You're sexy, Suzanne.' He had only very rarely used her full name. Somehow it emphasised the seriousness of what he was saying.

'Me? Sexy?' She gave a high laugh which sounded dangerously uncontrolled. 'Don't be ridiculous.' Nobody had ever called her sexy before. Her father had once told her that she was a very attractive little thing, but sexy? Angela and women like her were sexy—in their well-cut clothes, with their scarlet mouths and perfectly groomed features, perfectly groomed hair.

'It must have been the clothes,' she told him steadily. When she thought of herself, she thought of jeans and jumpers and hair everywhere. A grown-up tomboy. 'I won't wear anything like that again.'

'You mean you didn't like the attention?' His voice was husky and it made her feel hot, on fire.

'It was all right, I suppose,' she muttered, staring down at her feet in their high shoes. Even with heels, she realised, she was still inches shorter than he was.

'I got quite sick of some of the men telling me that you were a sight for sore eyes.'

'I'm sorry.' She wondered whether he was drunk, saying all these things to her. He didn't sound drunk, but there was an odd inflection in his voice and she sneaked a glance upward at him. 'Did *you* think that I was a sight for sore eyes?' she heard herself ask. 'Or just an embarrassing nuisance?' She couldn't bear the thought that she might have embarrassed him.

'What do you think?' Then he did something that made her feel dizzy. He placed his hands on the counter behind her, so that as he leant forward his face was only inches away from her own.

'The latter, I guess. After all, you're always telling me that I'm a child.'

'I take that back. Physically, you're a woman and a very desirable one.'

Their eyes met and she wanted him to kiss her so badly that when his mouth did find hers she hardly even felt a quiver of surprise. It just seemed that he was reacting to an unspoken urgency in her.

She didn't hesitate, not even for a fraction of a second. She reached up and wound her arms around his neck and returned his kiss with an explosion of feeling that half frightened her in its intensity.

He kept his hands on the counter, but his mouth pressed fiercely down on hers and his tongue explored and invaded with savage hunger.

When he straightened up, she felt for a moment that it was to draw back, but his hand found the nape of her neck and his fingers coiled into her hair and he pulled her towards him so that she could feel his body against hers, so close that it seemed as though they would fuse.

He was breathing thickly and so was she. His mouth left hers and she arched back, whimpering with pleasure as his teeth nipped against the column of her neck.

He untucked her blouse from the waistband of her skirt and slowly unbuttoned the front, still kissing her; then he pulled aside the blouse, groaning hoarsely when her breasts were exposed, full and heavy.

He covered one breast with his hand, caressing it, holding it up to his mouth, and she arched further back against the counter, expelling a long, shuddering sigh when the wetness of his tongue began flicking against the erect nipple. His mouth sucked hard on the throbbing peak, sending wave after wave of longing through her, then moved to explore the other, until both were raised and hard.

Her fingers fumbled to undo the buttons of his shirt because now the thin material was a barrier between them. She wanted, desperately, to feel the hardness of his flesh against hers, and when at last all the buttons were undone she realised that he must have been feeling the same as she, because he pulled her against him, so that her breasts were squashed against his broad chest.

He caressed her thighs, parting them, and then with his fingers he began doing things that no man had ever done to her before.

She had never conceived that desire could be as strong as this—a leashed animal that has broken its reins and is running wild and free.

He had slipped his hand inside her flimsy, lacy underwear—underwear which she had specially bought because it seemed to suit the wicked skimpiness of her attire.

Moistness filled her and spread outwards, an excited desire so strong that she would have collapsed onto the floor if he hadn't been supporting her with his arms.

His fingers moved with an easy, expert rhythm and every sensuous stroke heightened the numb longing inside her.

'This is madness,' she heard him mutter into her ear.

'Why?'

'Because I've known you for ever. We grew up together, for God's sake. I've always seen you as little Suzie Stanton, running wild on the estate. Never as a woman.'

'How many times do I have to tell you that I've grown up?' she asked fiercely. She smoothed her hands flat over his chest, feeling the muscular hardness with a quiver of excitement. She didn't want him to stop. She didn't want either of them to start thinking; she didn't want to break the momentum of what was happening between them. Some driving force inside her needed this in a way that defied rationality.

His mouth crushed hers, barely seeming to let her up for air, and she guided his hand back to her aching breasts, feeling weak as his fingers played with her nipples.

It baffled her that she could dislike him with such intensity one minute and yet, at the next, be drawn to him with a force that left her winded. How could the two be tied together?

Precisely how far they would have got in their love-making remained open for speculation because through the hazy mists she heard the voice at exactly the same time as he did, although their reactions were completely different.

'Hello-o-o...? Where are you, Dane? Dane...?'

It was so unexpected that Suzanne nearly jumped in shock. She pulled back, her face scarlet, and with shaking, hurried movements she began to straighten her clothes, feeling an overwhelming sense of guilt and horror.

Dane had straightened and was utterly calm and controlled. By the time Angela's footsteps were outside the kitchen door, Suzanne had managed to get herself into some semblance of order and was holding a plate in one hand and a dishcloth in the other, as though they helped to reinforce the image that nothing had been going on.

Angela's eyes at the kitchen door took them both in and there was a frozen, suspicious silence which Dane made no attempt to break, so that she was forced to say, with an attempt at lightness, that she had returned for her bag.

'The front door was open,' she said, focusing all her attention on Suzanne and none on Dane.

Suzanne blushed vividly and began to stammer something under her breath.

'And have you collected your bag?' Dane asked, his voice cool and unrevealing. He pushed himself away from the counter and strolled towards the other woman, taking his time, and Angela was forced to look at him, even though, Suzanne knew instinctively, she would rather have vented her considerable anger on her because Dane simply wasn't the sort you exploded with.

'Come with me,' he said, and he left the room, shutting the kitchen door quietly behind him.

Suzanne brushed down her skirt and brushed back her hair and wondered whether she should risk leaving the kitchen and sneaking back to her bedroom. She thought about it for what seemed like hours, half hoping that she would hear the front door slam, and in the end arrived at the conclusion that she couldn't wait for ever in the kitchen. They were hardly going to be standing outside the closed door, talking in hushed whispers, were they? And if they were she was certain that she would hear something. She tiptoed towards the door, pressed her ear against it, heard nothing, and very quietly let herself out.

They were in the sitting room and the door was shut. Whatever was going on, they wanted to make sure that they weren't overheard. Was Angela declaring her hand? Fighting for a man she considered hers? There had been nothing, apart from Suzanne's guilty face, to suggest that anything untoward had been taking place, but a guilty face would have been enough for Angela to assume the worst. In this case, it would be the truth.

She ran lightly back into her bedroom and as soon as she was in the safety of her locked room she removed the hateful clothes, stripping them off and hurling them into the corner. She never wanted to see them again. She could hardly believe that she had been so stupid as to have worn them in the first place. What had she been thinking of? How could she have been spurred into such foolish behaviour simply because Angela had told her that she would be better off serving drinks to the guests instead of mingling with them?

She had acted on impulse and now, lying in bed, she regretted every single minute of it, because Dane would never have been tempted by her if she hadn't displayed herself so blatantly. He would have continued looking at her as if she were his younger sister—someone, as he had said, whom he had known for ever, not someone with whom he would ever have been tempted to get involved.

He had touched her and she had responded with a fervour which filled her now with shame.

But she had to admit to herself, burning hotly in the silent, unlit bedroom, that she had had any number of opportunities to walk away. He would never have tried to stop her. She could have laughed and slithered out of his arms when he'd first kissed her; in fact she could have prevented that kiss from happening from the start. But she hadn't because she had wanted him and every other consideration had taken a back seat.

She hid her head under the pillow so that the little noises in the room—the ticking of the clock, the sound of the wind outside—became muffled and indistinct, leaving her to brood on the army of thoughts marching solidly along in her head, each one more graphic than the next.

She wished impotently for any number of things, but most of all she wished that Dane Sutherland had never re-entered her life, looking for a good cause to appease his conscience.

She had not realised until now just how vulnerable she still was when it came to him. As vulnerable, it seemed, as she had been years before when she had nurtured her hopeless, childish infatuation. She lay on the bed and relived that roller coaster of emotion that had plagued her in her adolescence. Had she really outgrown all that, she wondered, or had she just fondly imagined that she had?

It seemed useless to ponder about it, just as it was useless to try and pretend that nothing had happened between them. The only thing she could do would be to convince him that it had meant nothing to her—nothing at all.

If he said nothing to her, then she would not volunteer an apology as she had the last time. She would just remain silent and take her cue from him. If he mentioned it, she would admit that she had been attracted to him and would laugh it off lightly. He would understand that. Men understood simple things like physical desire; they appreciated the concept of abandoning all common sense when confronted by naked animal attraction.

She would never let him see that what she had felt had been much more than a brief lapse into passion. She closed her eyes and tried not to see it herself, but the idea, once implanted, had taken root, and when she finally fell asleep not long before dawn she had already reached the awful conclusion that what she felt for him now reached far beyond the tidy limits of infatuation. She was in love with him. In love with the one man she had once convinced herself that she hated.

Suzanne got up sluggishly the following morning, and the revelation, which she had hoped the night before, in a muddle-headed way, would fade in the same fashion as a nightmare fades on waking, was as stark as it had been then.

She was in love with Dane Sutherland. She was in love with a man who had briefly lost his senses and allowed himself to be drawn to a woman whom he still saw as a child, because she had been dressed provocatively.

She approached the kitchen with great hesitation and was sick with relief when she read the note on the table, the strong black writing telling her that he had been called away on business and wouldn't be back until the middle of the week.

What business? Angela business, perhaps?

Suzanne so successfully convinced herself that, wherever he was, he was in the company of the other woman that it was a shock to see her, efficient, cool-faced and as immaculately dressed as usual, at the office on the Monday morning.

Angela's office door, which was normally shut, was open, so that she could see anyone walking by, and Suzanne had a sinking feeling that she had been waiting— waiting for her to pass. Like a barracuda waiting to make a kill.

Suzanne looked in, because ignoring the open door and the pert blonde sitting eagle-eyed behind her desk would have been even more obvious, and nodded.

'Could you come in here, please?' Angela didn't bother to get out from behind the desk, nor did she attempt to disguise the hostility in her voice, and Suzanne reluctantly walked into the room, only shutting the door because she was told and not from choice.

'I expect you know what I want to talk to you about.'

Suzanne sat down, crossed her legs and looked at the other woman warily. 'Not really,' she said uncomfortably.

'Now, now,' Angela said with a reptilian smile, 'you don't really expect me to believe that you're that stupid, do you?'

'If this has to do with Saturday night...'

'This has everything to do with Saturday night. I'll

pass over the way you made a complete fool of yourself, preening and posing in that pathetic fancy dress you wore, for reasons which I can't begin to understand. Did you think that that was the only way that you would be able to attract a man like Dane?' She leant forward and Suzanne was immeasurably grateful for the desk separating them.

'I don't think that this is the right place to be having this sort of discussion,' she began, which, judging from Angela's reaction, was the last thing she should have said.

'I am in charge of this office,' she said with such hatred in her voice that Suzanne was silenced. 'You are little more than a charity case handed to me by Dane. Although, I suppose you have forgotten that little fact.'

'No, I am very much aware that he was kind enough to provide me...' Another mistake, she realised too late. She shouldn't have said anything at all.

'Yes, he was very kind, too kind, because kindness wasn't enough for you, was it? When did you decide that you wanted more than just a job and a roof over your head? When did you decide that because you knew him in the past that would be a good starting point to getting to know him a bit better—more than a bit better?'

'I never decided any such thing!' She could see dismissal staring her in the face, but she couldn't do a thing about it.

'You can stop lying right now!' Angela banged her fist down on the desk and her cup of coffee rattled in its saucer from the impact. 'You took one look at Dane and thought that you would be able to worm your way into his affections because he was stupid enough to feel sorry for you!'

'How dare you accuse me of something like that?' Suzanne's face was white, but even as she said it she knew the answer. Angela had dared because that was the only mode of behaviour that she could understand, because it was what she would have done herself. The question of love would never have entered her mind. Angela, Suzanne saw, wasn't in love with Dane Sutherland. She wanted him and all the things that he carried with him: his money, his style, his power. She wanted to bask in his reflected glory.

'Because it's the truth! I can see straight through you and I have done ever since I laid eyes on that innocent, lost-little-girl look. What did it feel like when you realised that you weren't going to get anywhere with him? When you realised that he just isn't attracted to lost little girls?'

She paused after that, and Suzanne wondered whether that was a question in search of an answer.

'Dane Sutherland wants a woman,' Angela spat out, her face distorted with ugly emotion. 'He doesn't want a child!'

'In that case, why are you overreacting to the situation? What have you got to fear from me, since he could never be attracted to me in a month of Sundays?' Sure dismissal now, she thought. Out on my ear, probably without the pay packet that's due to me.

'Is that when you decided that the only way to get him would be to dress like a tart?'

That stung. It brought a red flush to Suzanne's cheeks, and she could see the other woman looking at her with narrow-eyed comprehension.

'That just isn't true!'

'Do you imagine that because he made a pass at you in a kitchen, when he was in no fit state, you now have what you want?'

'We weren't...' Suzanne began, faltering and then taking a deep breath because she just couldn't continue with the lie that they had not been doing anything.

'You will never get what you want. Dane may have

been attracted to you because you crooked your finger—
and what man wouldn't take what's offered on a
plate?—but you're nothing to him. Do you understand?
Dane and I understand one another. And I intend to have
him.'

Suzanne stood up. She was surprised that she hadn't
been given the sack. Perhaps refusing to sit silent and
be insulted by one's boss wasn't a sackable offence. Perhaps, and this only came to her late, when she was back
at her desk and trying to get stuck into her work, Angela
couldn't sack her, even though she desperately wanted
to. Perhaps her hands were tied.

Angela wanted Dane; she intended, she had said, to
have him. There was nothing going on. Yet.

Suzanne shivered. Somewhere in that beautiful head
a screw was loose, and that, more than anything else,
made Angela a dangerous foe.

CHAPTER SEVEN

SUZANNE didn't see Dane until the end of the week. She had waited with a sense of sick anticipation for him to return on the Wednesday evening, and had gone to bed at ten o'clock with a feeling of disappointment, which she'd told herself was not an appropriate thing to feel. Not when she had made her mind up to be as distant with him as possible.

So on the Thursday, when there was no sign of him, she cheerfully told herself that she was not at all disappointed but rather relieved, in fact. She went to bed with a book, fell asleep with it on her stomach with the side-light still on, and promptly had a very vivid dream which involved her, Dane and Angela in some nightmarish triangle, the details of which she could hardly remember when she awoke in the morning.

It was only a matter of accident when she did see him the following day. She had just finished washing up the one dish from her supper and was about to retire to bed when she heard the front door open and close, and despite her gay self-assurances that the lapse had restored all of her self-control she felt her stomach go into a tight knot, and every muscle in her body turned rigid.

She hurriedly left the kitchen and confronted him head-on. He was rolling up the sleeves of his shirt and if her sudden appearance in his path had taken him by surprise he gave no indication of it. He continued doing what he was doing, not looking at her after the first

glance, and after flirting with the idea of heading off to
her bedroom she said politely, 'How did your trip go?'

He looked at her more fully this time. 'Good. Very
good. More than worth the months of effort that have
been put into this particular deal. At long last, things are
beginning to fall into place. America, little Suzie, was
an interlude. You're always so curious about it. Let me
just say that, as things are turning out, my self-imposed
exile will have been worth it.' He smiled slowly, without
amusement, then said, changing the subject and striding
into the kitchen, 'Any coffee lying about?'

'Is it to do with Martha?' she asked, off the top of
her head, and he shot her a speculative look.

'Oh, yes,' he said softly, 'it's to do with Martha. Now,
back to my question. Any coffee?'

'Hot, freshly brewed and waiting to be poured into a
cup? Surprisingly enough, no.' He had, his face showed,
already said enough on the subject of Martha, and she
was still too sensitive after what had happened between
them to prod him further.

He laughed with his back to her. 'And could I persuade you to make me one?'

'Oh, I don't think so,' Suzanne said thoughtfully, relieved that he hadn't mentioned that dreadful episode,
and more than prepared to have their relationship return
to its normal, politely friendly basis. 'But, if you're making, you could make one for me as well.'

And ten minutes later she found herself sitting at the
kitchen table opposite him, cradling a mug of coffee in
her hands. It felt dangerously domestic to be sitting here
with him, wearing her oldest clothes and no make-up at
all, and listening to him talk to her.

He told her about New York, amused because she
hung onto every word. He described it with dry wit,
telling her about places she had only ever heard of, because holidays abroad had been as inaccessible as trips

to the moon. Her father would never have been able to afford a holiday to America, of all places, and hearing Dane talk about it gave her a vicarious thrill. There was no more mention of his stepmother or of what his dealings had to do with her.

'You're doing a very dangerous thing sitting there,' he said, shooting her a crooked smile and looking at her in that way that he had—as though he could see right into the core of her.

'What's that?'

'You're stroking my ego with your attentiveness.' He leant forward with his elbows on the table, in the same way as she was sitting staring at him. 'Didn't your father ever tell you that such attention can be very disturbing?'

'No.' Should she take him seriously? The question threw her into a turmoil of confusion. 'Of course he didn't. He was embarrassed enough telling me about the birds and the bees when I was fourteen. Of course, I already knew all about that.'

'Of course.' There was amusement in the depths of his grey eyes.

'From friends.'

'Indeed.'

'Stop staring at me like that,' she said, clearing her throat and risking a direct look at his face. He hadn't shaved. There was a dark shadow along his jawline which she only now noticed.

'I've discovered that I rather like staring at you.'

She gave a nervous laugh and stood up.

'Where are you going?' he asked. 'Have I embarrassed you?' He stood up with her and she could hear the amusement in his voice.

Her whole body was tingling and she had to force her legs to move in the direction of the door.

'To bed,' she said with her back to him, in what she hoped was a carefree voice. 'And no, you haven't.'

Lying, she was finding out, was becoming something of a habit as far as he was concerned. Every time he asked her a personal question, in fact.

'What a good idea,' he said lazily, following her out of the kitchen. 'And I'm glad to hear it, even though I suspect you're lying.' He gave a deep-throated chuckle.

'You have a hugely inflated ego,' she told him, aware that he was following her and wondering what exactly he proposed to do when they arrived at her bedroom door. He hadn't entered her bedroom once since she had moved in, and she couldn't see him doing it now, whatever peculiar, flirtatious mood he seemed to be in. 'Why do you think that every word you say sends me into a dither?'

'Because that transparent face of yours gives you away every time.'

They reached the door and she stood with her back to it and looked at him. 'I do not get into a dither every time you speak to me,' she told him evenly. 'You do not qualify as some dark, disturbing stranger who's swept into my life on a white stallion. I've known you off and on for longer than I care to remember. You just need to put a brake on your imagination.'

There, that sounded remarkably well controlled. Articulate, even. It irritated her that that half-smile was still playing on his lips, but she reasoned that he would be the last person in the world to admit to having made an error of judgement when it came to someone else's character.

'I shall have a good talking to with my hugely inflated ego tonight.' He grinned.

'I realise that you're probably accustomed to women throwing themselves at you every time you put one foot forward, but please don't cast me in the same role.'

'Not even after what happened after the party?'

There was a tense little silence and Suzanne felt behind her back for the doorknob.

'I would rather not mention that at all.'

'I'm sure you wouldn't,' he agreed.

He wasn't smiling any longer, which was even more disturbing because now there was no screen over the lazy, blatant sexuality in his grey eyes.

She turned the doorknob and slipped inside the bedroom, which instantly made her feel safer.

'You're not ending this conversation yet, are you, Suzie? Just when it's getting started?'

She felt her heart give a bit of a lurch, but her voice was steady enough when she replied. 'I'm tired. It's been a long week.'

That, at any rate, was the truth. Angela had not descended on her with any more accusations, but Suzanne had still found herself keeping a cautious watch on the door to her office, waiting for it to open and reveal 'the vampire' in all her glory.

She hadn't told Robert anything of their conversation, but he had gleaned from her expression on her return to her desk that all was not right, and the vampire description had been his. Since then he had brought in several bulbs of garlic, which he had distributed in the pot plants, much to Suzanne's amusement.

She decided that Dane would not relish the thought of his top executive, whose abilities he doubtless admired even if her physique didn't enter into the equation, being elevated to the position of the Evil One.

'Hasn't it, though?' He wasn't budging and eventually she began to close the bedroom door.

She wasn't expecting him to push it open and stride past her into the room, which was what he did. She stared at him open-mouthed and asked him what he thought he was doing, to which, naturally, he had the perfect reply.

'Inspecting what you've done with the room.' He was looking around him, noting the various bits and pieces which she had excavated from storage and now displayed on the mantelpiece of the fireplace and on the window-ledges: framed photographs, a few ornaments, most of which were tasteless in the extreme—cheap souvenirs of day trips to places like Bournemouth and Brighton—but which held a great deal of sentimental value.

'I haven't done anything with it,' she said, keeping her position near the door, her arms folded.

'It looks more lived in than the bedsit did from what I saw of it.' He paused in front of a photo of her father and her, taken years before in happier times.

'I've brought out more of my personal things.'

He moved on from the photo and stopped in front of a Mexican ornament which she had found in a charity shop and bought for her father for his birthday a decade ago. He held it, looked at it, and she waited patiently by the door, wondering how much more lingering he intended to do in the bedroom.

'If you want to do anything more dramatic with the room,' he said suddenly, 'then by all means feel free.' He waved his hand vaguely to encompass the bedroom. 'It's somewhat on the bland side.'

'Oh, it suits me the way it is!' Suzanne exclaimed, shocked. What did he mean by anything more dramatic? Black walls and striped window-sills? 'I'm not a dramatic person. I would feel uncomfortable in a dramatic room.'

He was watching her closely as she spoke, and now he strolled slowly towards her. Since she was standing close to the door, she hoped that this signalled his exit, but he stopped in front of her and eventually she said brusquely, 'You're on your way out, I take it? The door's right there.'

'You always seem to fold your arms whenever you're talking to me. A psychologist would have a field-day with that little trait.' He reached out and grasped her wrists, bringing her arms down to her sides.

'What are you doing?'

'When you stand with your arms crossed like that, it looks as though you're warding off an attack. Or else you feel ashamed of your body. Which is it?' He was grinning but there was something else there too, lurking in the depths of his eyes.

'Should I fear anything from you?' she asked, nervously licking her lips. 'I don't, anyway,' she continued quickly, just in case he came up with a retort to that one. 'And I'm not in the least bit ashamed of my body. I admit that I wasn't too happy with the way I looked when I moved up to London, but I've lost that weight now.' She would have folded her arms again if they hadn't still been pinned to her side. 'I shall never be small and delicate, but that doesn't bother me.' She lifted her chin and looked at him and her eyes seemed to ask whether it bothered him.

'Of course not; why should it bother you? I've never felt the slightest inclination to be small and delicate either.' Which made her laugh.

'No, I don't suppose the women in your life would appreciate that.' It was as well, she thought, to remind him that there was someone else involved. It was as well to introduce a touch of reality because feeling him close to her like this was doing dangerous things to her equilibrium.

'There are no women in my life at the moment,' he said softly.

'Oh, I see,' Suzanne said, when she didn't see at all. Or not much anyway. 'And Angela?'

'Ah, yes, Angela. You've been hinting long enough about that. There's nothing going on between us. I respect her business skills, which is why I brought her over with me.'

'Hasn't it occurred to you that she might have been harbouring a different idea?'

His lips thinned, but he smiled. 'I've set her right on that count,' was all he said, but it was enough.

Enough, she thought frantically, to make me deliriously happy. It doesn't mean a thing, of course; it doesn't mean that he's done anything ridiculous like fall madly in love with me. Good grief, I can't see that happening in a month of Sundays, but I'm still happy.

'What a foolish idea that we were involved.' He raised one hand and stroked the side of her face and she felt heat flare under the trail of his finger. 'She's a good worker but do you really imagine that she was my type? Still, I should have seen the danger signals earlier on. I thought that I was doing her a favour in giving her the biggest job of her career. Unfortunately she read more into the offer than was there.'

'Poor Angela.' Suzanne could almost begin to feel slightly sorry for the other woman.

'No need to feel sorry for her,' he said, reading her mind. 'Her stint here will look very good on her CV.'

'You mean she's leaving?'

'Her choice, not mine.' His finger had moved from her cheek to her mouth, then back to her cheek, and she could feel her heart pounding.

'But I thought that she loved the job.'

'Alas, dear Angela realised that she wasn't going to get what she had more or less banked on getting, which was me.' His eyes hardened and this time she felt quite a bit sorrier for the other woman.

'And I thought that women were the guilty ones when it came to leading men up garden paths.'

'I never told Angela that what we had was ever anything more than a business relationship. Was it my fault that she misread the signals?'

'Oh, no,' Suzanne muttered sarcastically, curving her fingers around his wrists and pulling his hands down to his sides. 'I can see that you're utterly blameless in this—as pure, in fact, as the driven snow.'

'Oh, good,' he told her. 'I'm glad that you see my point of view.'

Suzanne opened her lips to protest, but before she could say a word his mouth descended, covering hers, and he pinned her back against the wall. For an instant she responded with hot, enthusiastic passion, then she struggled against him, pushing him back.

'What,' she said unsteadily, 'do you think you're doing?'

He reached out and leant his hands on the wall behind her, encircling her so that she was obliged to look up at him.

'What I have wanted to do for quite some time now.'

'Don't be silly,' she said on a desperate note.

He traced the outline of her face with his finger and didn't say anything. His hand moved to her collar-bone and the feel of that feathery touch along her skin, following the line of her shirt collar, made her weak.

'I'm not about to become another Dane Sutherland trophy before you tire of me as well and decide to move on!'

'I want you, Suzie.'

'You can't just have everything you want!'

'And you want me.'

'You're not listening to a word I'm saying!'

'I can feel it when I touch you.' As if to demonstrate his point, he slowly unbuttoned her shirt and exposed her breasts which were heaving underneath the lacy trappings of her bra.

'Please, Dane, I think you ought to leave before we

both do something we'll regret in the morning.' What a cliché. It could have come straight out of a third-rate movie. She fumbled, trembling, with the front of her blouse and his hands covered hers.

'How could we regret something that we both want?'

'I don't believe in casual affairs, Dane. I wasn't brought up that way. I know that that probably sounds very unsophisticated to you, but that's just the way it is.'

'So your plan is to keep yourself in pristine condition until Mr Right comes along, whenever that may be. Always hoping, of course, that he is Mr Right, because, in case it's escaped you, people aren't always what they appear to be. You only need to look at the divorce rate to realise that.'

'Is that a case for hopping into bed with any and everyone?' she asked, drawing away from him and walking towards the window.

'Why do you think that the alternative to celibacy is promiscuity? I enjoy sex,' he said, strolling towards her and standing behind her, following her eyes down to the dark gardens below, 'but that doesn't mean that I spend all my free time trying to get women to climb into bed with me.'

'Not that you'd have to try very hard.'

'I'm not into chasing women, nor am I into collecting trophies. I don't personally think that that's either a desirable or a healthy lifestyle. On the other hand, when two people get along—even if it isn't love—and they want to sleep together, then why the hell not?'

He made it sound so sensible. He made it sound as if any disagreement with this morally persuasive train of reasoning was tantamount to insanity.

'Except that people get hurt, don't they?'

'And they don't get hurt when there's a wedding ring sealing the relationship?' He laughed, and there was a cynical edge to his laughter. 'That's not romantic, Suzie, it's downright naïve.'

'That's me,' she said coldly. 'Downright naïve.'

Or, to put it even more basically, she thought to herself, utterly stupid. Dane Sutherland was one of life's great manipulators. He was charming, sexy, intelligent, rich. He could manipulate most people to do things that they would probably never have dreamt up on their own. It might have been true enough that he had never encouraged Angela, but he had obviously admired her working abilities enough to bring her across to London to resurrect the semi-dead company in which he had invested his money, and deep down he must have known that a relationship other than strictly business was at the back of the other woman's mind.

Did he imagine that falling back on the technical argument that he had never promised anything would prove his innocence?

'Don't you believe in marriage at all?' she asked him. 'Your father had a very happy marriage before—'

'That's it precisely, though, isn't it? It proves my point even better. My father had had the experience of one good marriage behind him, yet he went ahead with blinding stupidity and got himself involved with a woman much younger than he was, who was clearly only after what his bank balance could offer.' There was a tightness in his voice and she could imagine that he had stiffened a little.

'He made a mistake.'

'Which generally happens when you let your heart rule your head.'

'How cold. So you intend to give the institution a miss just because your father made a mistake?'

'I never said that I intended to give the institution of marriage a miss,' he corrected her mildly. 'I merely don't intend to rush into it because I happen to find a woman desirable.'

Suzanne turned around so that she was half-perched on the window-sill and looking at him. She didn't want to have to watch that dark, angular, thrilling face, but it was difficult conducting a conversation with a disembodied voice coming from somewhere behind her. Especially a conversation which was making her angry.

'And when do you propose to rush into it?' she asked with polite disdain.

'When someone suitable comes along; when I can make an unhurried, clear-headed decision that that someone is a woman who can make herself useful to the kind of lifestyle that I lead.'

'Oh, I'm so impressed by your logical way of going about things, Dane. Will this suitable woman have to fill out any forms? Will she need character references?'

'Don't be ridiculous.'

'I'm not being ridiculous, you are.'

'Someone suitable', she thought. She knew what that meant. Someone elegant, good-looking, with the right background. A thoroughbred horse, all credentials in full working order. In other words, someone who stood at the opposite end of the spectrum to her. What he wanted from her was a brief, satisfactory fling. How sweet of him to make no bones about it.

'Don't tell me that you don't intend having sex with a man unless marriage is on the agenda.'

'That is precisely what I mean. I can't think of anything more distasteful than throwing myself into bed with a man simply for the temporary fun of it.'

'What's the matter with a bit of fun?' He was beginning to sound a trifle on the impatient side now. Soon, she supposed, impatience would give way to boredom, when he realised that he wasn't going to get anywhere with her. He would shrug his shoulders and walk away, knowing, no doubt, that he could find any number of drop-dead gorgeous women who would be only too glad to satisfy his desire for a bit of fun. And maybe some of them wouldn't want anything permanent out of it either.

She couldn't deny that the fun he dangled in front of her would be the substance of a lifetime's worth of memories for her, but did she really want to find herself a hopeless spinster in the years to come, sadly clutching her memories, unable to give herself to another man because no one could occupy the space that Dane Sutherland had been willing to fill for a short space of time?

Because that, she knew, was what would happen. She was in love with him and she would only love him harder if she went to bed with him. If she stayed away, she might regret it, but she would eventually meet someone else and that element of comparison, at least, would not have to be dealt with. It all made tremendous sense to her.

'When does Angela intend to leave?' she asked, thinking it wise to change the conversation. She could feel her nails digging into her arms just as she could feel his strong, mesmeric presence trying to engulf her.

'I've told her that she can take her time, but I doubt she'll stay longer than a couple of months. She has good contacts in America. She should be able to find a job without any difficulty. And of course I shall give her an impeccable reference.'

'What a kind gesture. But then,' she said acidly, 'you do specialise in kind gestures if it means alleviating your conscience.'

'Oh, for God's sake!' He ran his fingers through his hair and looked at her with restless irritation which pleased rather than depressed her. She only wished that she could rifle through her mind and come up with a few more remarks guaranteed to needle. It just wasn't fair that she should feel this way about this man. 'I thought we had put that particular one to rest, Suzie.'

'I'm sure you have.'

'But *you* haven't, is that it? You still want to put me in the role of the traitor.'

'I don't want to put you in any role,' she said sweetly. 'I'm merely pointing out that there are a few cracks in this wonderful portrait you want to paint of yourself as the world's greatest benefactor.'

He smiled at her. It was such a disconcerting reaction to what she had just said that she couldn't think where she had reached in her argument or, for that matter, where she should go from here. She just knew that that smile was doing catastrophic things to her composure.

'Next you'll be trying to convince me that you deserve a sainthood, I suppose,' she continued, stubbornly refusing to let him see how much he was now getting under her skin.

He continued smiling and raised his eyebrows in expectation of further developments of this line of argument.

'And it is not funny!' she burst out, wondering whether this was part of his plan to throw her completely.

'No, you're absolutely right, it's not in the least funny. However, you might like to know that you look extremely sexy when you're in a rage.'

And you look extremely sexy all of the time, she thought in a dazed way.

She wondered fleetingly why she was bothering to hold out against his considerable charm. Who cared? She had said that she would never make love with a man unless she was in love with him, and she wouldn't be deserting that principle. Did it matter that she would end up being hurt? Wasn't she hurting now? More to the point, did she want her epitaph to read 'Lonely spinster who stupidly never gave in'?

'I wouldn't be in a rage if you hadn't waltzed into my bedroom without my consent.'

'*My* bedroom,' he corrected her.

'Oh, all right, your bedroom. Technically speaking. I do live here, though, in case you'd forgotten. At your behest, no less. I'm entitled to some privacy.'

'Not when I want to make love to you.'

Stay calm, she told herself with a drowning feeling. Hang on to your blood pressure. Try to ignore that gleam in his eyes. Get through this and you can get through anything.

'Can't you take no for an answer?' she asked with a sensation of panic.

'I don't recall offhand ever being in that position.'

'You're the most vain person I've ever met in my life!' she exclaimed, and he laughed and continued looking at her.

'And you're awfully predictable. Tell me now that I'm not throwing you into a dither.'

She didn't answer. She didn't think that she could formulate a lie with any kind of coherence. She just wished desperately that he would go, because she could feel the arguments made rationally in her head a while back going down the proverbial pan. She was so vastly turned on by him that even breathing was getting to be a bit of a strain.

'Tell me now that you don't want me,' he said in a lower, softer, more insinuating voice, and when she didn't answer that either, because her tongue appeared to have worked its way to the roof of her mouth and was finding it impossible to move, he held her face in his hands again and bent his head very slowly down to hers.

He kissed her gently, exploring her mouth, tasting her

with the thoroughness of the connoisseur sampling some heavenly vintage.

No struggle now. She curved her arms around his neck and was the one to deepen the kiss. He was still kissing her when he carried her to the bed, only stopping when his lips moved on, searching out new territory to set ablaze.

He unbuttoned her shirt and through the lace of her bra his tongue flirted with her nipples, which hardened under the teasing caress.

Then, when she thought that she was reaching a stage of unbearable anticipation, he disposed of her bra and she felt the wetness of his mouth surround the tight peaks of her breasts, and she pressed his head against her so that her whole body was filled with a torrent of desire that was beyond thought.

She tugged his shirt out of the waistband of his trousers and ran her hands along the base of his back. She could feel the hard muscles under her fingers and she pushed her fingers just under the top of the waistband.

With a groan that was a mixture of heat and urgency, he unzipped his trousers and discarded them. She heard them drop to the ground.

In this vortex of passion that he had led her to, every sound, every movement seemed to be magnified a thousandfold.

As he licked and caressed his way down, down to her stomach, arousing her with his leisurely exploration, she felt the moistness between her legs waiting to surround him, and it was a relief when he eased her trousers off her.

Through half-opened eyes, she watched the dark head find its way to her womanhood, and then she closed her eyes because now she could do nothing but get lost in the exquisite sensation taking her over. She didn't want to see, or think. She just wanted to feel.

His hands caressed her thighs and his tongue tasted the sweetness that seemed produced for him only. She sighed and moaned and heard these little sounds of pleasure in a way that was almost disembodied, hearing them but not hearing them, aware that she had quite lost control.

He straightened up and guided her hand to the evidence of his desire and she felt a surge of excitement fill her.

It was only when he moved against her that excitement was replaced by panic and the rational arguments which had taken a back seat reared up with affront.

She saw in a blinding flash how her life would be mapped out if she let him make love to her, if she let him complete his masterful conquest of her body.

Was this what it was like when people said that they had seen their lives flash before their eyes in an instant? she thought. It must be. Except what had flashed before her eyes hadn't been her past, it had been her future.

She was in love with him now, but if she let this happen she would not only still be in love with him, she would be his and he would know it. She would become helpless and impotent against the addiction of being with him, and when the time came for him to abandon her, which it inevitably would, she would have nothing to fall back on, not even her dignity.

She had a very vivid image of herself trailing behind him like a miserable, whipped dog, waiting for any little favour that he would care to hand out, except that by then he would probably be too irritable with her devotion to hand out anything at all.

But how could she not turn into some pathetic creature living each day with the fear that it might be last, as far as Dane Sutherland was concerned? Falling in love with him had been fairly pathetic as it was. Making love to him could only compound the already complicated issue.

Because, however much he wanted a dalliance with her, he would never marry her and it was just not in her to sustain a relationship with a man who had no intention of tying the knot at some point in time.

And the only point in time that she could see them heading towards was the point in time when he became fed up with her, and then he would merely inform her in that dry, cold voice of his that he had never made promises.

'I'm sorry,' she said huskily. 'I can't.'

She thought that he hadn't heard her at first because he made no effort to create distance between them, so she said sharply, 'No!' which did stop him.

His head jerked up and he looked her in the eyes.

'No? No? What do you mean, no?'

'I mean that I can't go through with this. I'm sorry.' She averted her face and he dragged it round with his fingers so that she had to look at him, albeit reluctantly.

'Of course you're joking.'

'I can't make love to you. I thought that I could because you were so persuasive and I am attracted to you, but—'

'I will not be blackmailed into marriage,' he grated, 'if that's the game you're playing.'

'I wasn't trying to blackmail you into anything!'

It felt very cold now that they were no longer clasped in an embrace, and she sat up and drew the covers around her.

'There's a name for women like you,' he said cuttingly, standing up and shoving on his trousers but not bothering with his shirt. She looked at the bronzed, powerful torso and looked away quickly.

'I'm sorry,' was all she could whisper. She could feel tears springing to the corners of her eyes and she blinked them away rapidly.

She half wanted to throw everything away and plead

CATHY WILLIAMS   135

with him to stay after all, but she didn't. Instead she stared down in silence at the covers spread around her and was only aware that the room was once again empty when she heard the bedroom door slam so hard that it made the window-panes rattle.

Then she gave a deep sigh, lay back down on the pillow and wept.

CHAPTER EIGHT

IT IS VERY difficult to measure the change in a person's attitude. If she had sat down with a pencil and paper and tried to make a coherent list, she would not have known where to start, but Suzanne could feel the change that had now shifted the footing of their relationship as acutely as if Dane had suddenly transformed from Dr Jekyll into Mr Hyde.

Over the next two weeks she rarely saw him, and when she did there was no overt hostility in his attitude, no aggrieved coldness, more a kind of shuttered politeness that was more cutting than outright anger.

When he addressed her, and that was something which he appeared to do on the move, standing up, virtually heading for the door as he spoke, it was with a courtesy that had something deadly in it. She hated to think that she would never see that driving need in his eyes again, or be the butt of his teasing or even listen to the dry, witty way that he spoke about most things, as though his perspective on life was that of amused spectator, watching and taking it all in.

When she had had all that at her disposal, when she had been wrapped up in her frantic world of hot and cold whenever he was around, angry and disturbed one minute, charmed the next, it had never occurred to her just how much she would miss it if it was taken away. Now he had taken it away and she was realising just how acutely deprived she felt at the loss.

And that had nothing to do with the physical side of things. She missed seeing him, being able to look at him, indulging her fascination with his body. Did he miss her too? she wondered. At all? Did the image of her occasionally flit through his mind or had he been able to write her off without too much undue trouble?

The problem was that whenever she asked herself questions like these the answers that flew into her head weren't the ones that she wanted, but from the way he acted toward her she couldn't escape the fact that he was a man who was busily getting on with his life and not a man trying to conceal a still burning flame of hunger for her.

It was only when she lay in bed at night, with her eyes shut, that she could give in to a few private fantasies about him. In her fantasies he was always doing something utterly out of keeping with his character, like breaking down her bedroom door and declaring undying love. In all of them, he was transformed into a man who was a shadow of his former self—composure, self-control, arrogance, all thrown by the wayside because he was eaten away by love. Then, when she would see him the next day for three minutes on his way out, she would realise that his composure, his self-control, his arrogance were all as intact as they had ever been.

So she began working much longer hours than she had done previously, simply to be out of the apartment, and she also began spending far more of her time digging into other files when her own assigned work was finished. She rummaged around in filing cabinets and in the empty office, deserted by Robert who felt that any overtime was a serious encroachment on his valuable arguing time with his girlfriend, read all about acquisitions which had not materialised, deals held in pending. She even unearthed Angela's forecasts for the company for the year ahead, the details of which Angela had

handed to Suzanne and Robert in skeleton form, probably because she considered them too insignificant in the
company to be shown much more than that.

It all helped to take her mind off Dane. She found the
solitude of the office quite soothing and it was interesting to investigate work not directly related to what she
was doing. There was nothing wrong in what she was
doing, but there was a clandestine pleasure in it, and she
doubted that she would have attempted to rifle through
the filing cabinets with quite so much impunity if Angela
had been on the scene. But she never was. Nothing had
been said to either of them or, as far as Suzanne was
aware, to anyone in the office about impending departure, but clearly Angela no longer saw much point to
killing herself in a job from which she had effectively
been sacked.

If Angela needed to put in extra time, she came in
very early. Suzanne knew that because she had come in
at six-thirty once herself, after a particularly unsatisfac-
tory night, and the other woman had been there, busy at
her desk. She hadn't seen Suzanne go by and Suzanne
had not made her presence known.

In her growing absorption with musty files, avidly
read in the silent office, came the bombshell, and to begin with it never even struck her that what she was holding was a stick of dynamite.

What caught her curiosity was the fact that the file
was heavily incomplete. It had none of the usual company records and details of conversations and letters
from financial directors and banks, just a few basic en-
tries in Angela's handwriting, and she got the uneasy
feeling that what she was looking at on a Friday evening,
at eight-thirty, when everyone else her age was probably
out drinking and celebrating the end of the week, was
not meant for her eyes.

In fact, she got the uneasy feeling that the file was not

actually meant for the filing cabinet at all. If it were, it certainly hadn't been filed by Angela, who never reduced herself to mundane tasks like that but sent her secretary skittering off to do them. It hadn't even been filed in any sort of logical manner and she wouldn't have come upon it if she hadn't seen it stuffed at the back when she'd pulled the drawer open. Whoever had rammed it in there had missed the drawer completely and it had fallen behind, wedged between the back of the drawer and the wall.

It couldn't have been Joan, the secretary, whose precision was legendary, so it could only have been the dim-witted temp who had worked with them for two days before being summarily dismissed by Angela for incompetence.

Suzanne could remember the girl in detail because she had actually rather liked her. Tall, outspoken, and sharp in a streetwise sort of way. Julia Fernes. But Angela had disliked her on sight, and had not taken too many pains to keep her thoughts to herself when it had come to sacking her.

'Noisy', was one of the labels she had used in that semi-patronising voice of hers, 'and not quite up to dealing with the level of work given to her'. Suzanne had heard the whole conversation to the agency while she had been sitting by Angela's desk, waiting to go through some accounts.

Maybe the file had been stuffed down there in a fit of spite. Could have been worse. Julia could have dismembered the computer system. Suzanne gazed up from the file and spent a minute or so musing with delight on Angela's reaction if their computer system had been wrecked.

She didn't get back that evening until after ten, to an empty flat, which remained empty for the weekend, and to fill her time she worked—back at the office, to which she had access using her coded pass card. It was a privilege given only to those in the management division and one which she had not exercised before.

It took her five hours of checking and a few phone calls to realise that the company didn't exist. It had been created. And it took her five minutes to realise that if she wanted to find an answer to that sticky problem she would have to penetrate the inner sanctum of Angela's office. Which she did, but with the tiptoeing caution of a child entering a room which, though not strictly forbidden, didn't have a welcome mat outside it either.

Angela kept her office the way she kept herself—extremely ordered, very tidy. An impeccably groomed office. The two plants were made out of silk and there were no personal touches anywhere to be seen.

There was also no information to be found in either of the two low black wooden filing cabinets which formed part of the office furniture. And over the next week what had started off as a bit of a puzzle developed into an addictive conundrum which had to be solved at all costs.

Suzanne was all dressed—jeans, man's loose-fitting striped shirt, weathered knapsack over shoulder—on Saturday morning to pursue the conundrum in the quiet confines of the office, and was drinking a cup of coffee standing up by the kitchen counter, when Dane walked in.

She hadn't seen him for the entire week, and seeing him now, when for once he hadn't been on her mind, made her suddenly nervous in a way that she heartily wished she wasn't, simply because it showed her how vulnerable she still was to him.

He was as taken aback by seeing her as she was by seeing him, although he recovered quickly and moved to make himself some coffee. A few weeks ago he would have asked her to make him one but there was no such familiarity now.

'Off somewhere?' he asked politely, glancing across at her briefly before settling himself down at the kitchen table and opening the newspaper.

Suzanne looked at his loose-limbed perfection and forgot the conundrum. Couldn't he even give her the time of day now? Had all his charm been for the sake of trying to get her to climb into bed with him? The thought filled her with sudden anger.

'Work, actually,' she said stiffly.

There was an inarticulate grunt while he continued to scour the newspaper and sip his coffee. He didn't even bother to look up at her.

'Thank you for taking such an interest,' she said coldly.

He took his time. He stopped reading the front page, which carried the usual headlines of death and government bungles, and sat back in his chair, crossing his long legs. Then he looked at her—possibly for the first time, she thought, since he had stormed out of her room, white-faced with rage.

'Is this what you want, Suzie?' he enquired baldly. 'My undivided attention and a feigned interest in how you're spending your Saturday?'

'Oh, forget it,' she muttered, dumping her cup in the sink and washing it. She turned back round to face him and he was still watching her, his eyes brooding, his mouth unsmiling.

'Like all women,' he drawled, 'you're cut to the quick to think that I'm not wringing my hands in despair over you.'

'Of course not!' she denied, but two patches of colour had appeared on her cheeks.

'Were you hoping that I would try and force entry into your bedroom?'

'I'm going.' She went to walk past him and he caught her wrist in his hand, though he remained where he was, sitting on the chair.

'Why are you going to work, Suzie?' he asked, and after what he had just said she seriously doubted that there was an atom of genuine interest in the question.

'Because the atmosphere there is healthier than the atmosphere around here,' she said bluntly.

'You made your position clear. No bed without love and marriage. So, please—' his mouth twisted coldly '—spare me the female pique.'

Through this icy little delivery the one desperate wish Suzanne had was that he were not holding her hand.

'I might have guessed,' she said without much care as to how she chose her words, 'that once my usefulness in appeasing your conscience as a rescued damsel in distress had worn off, and the potential bed-partner idea had to be ditched, that anything I said or did would be utterly irrelevant to you.'

'Poor little Suzie,' he said, dropping her hand so that she immediately wished that he hadn't. 'Would you like me to be a father-figure now to you?'

She looked away, unable to get her mind around the concept of that one. Father-figure? That would be like asking him to play Father Christmas in the local panto-mime. Dane Sutherland and father-figure just did not combine. They could hardly be uttered in the same breath.

Yet, in a way, perhaps he had put his finger on it. She had grown accustomed to his questions, to the way he'd listened whenever she'd said something to him, his eyes slanting across to her. He had been the first person since her father had died to really listen to what she had to say, and it was wounding to think that the only reason he had done it had been that he had wanted to seduce her eventually.

'I'm stupid; I shouldn't have said that.'

He clasped his hands behind his head and looked at her without saying anything and without giving anything away. His eyes were absolutely fathomless.

She nervously twirled her fingers in her hair, thought better of the gesture and replaced it with the equally nervous one of fidgeting.

'I miss talking to you,' she heard herself confess with horror. 'Do you miss talking to me?'

This, she thought, was what love and desperation made you do: say things that were better left unsaid, give yourself away in a million little gestures, a thousand little changes of expression.

'So why are you going to work today?'

If he had had a hundred years to think of something to say that would indicate to her how much her remark had displeased him, then that was it. She was a bore to him now. A few more outbursts about how much she missed talking to him—God, how could she have been so stupid?—and she would sink into the category of nuisance.

'Working on something,' she said, straightening and doing her best to get herself together.

'What?'

Suzanne shrugged, but her expression had changed from embarrassment to wariness. 'Oh, this and that; nothing much.'

'What are you hiding from me?'

His voice was suddenly sharp in the quiet of the kitchen—sharp enough for her to take a couple of steps backwards. There was no point in voicing any of her suspicion to him until everything had been checked out.

'Nothing,' she said quickly.

'Sure you're going to work?' he asked, swerving away

from the topic with a speed that left her momentarily breathless. 'No need to feel embarrassed if you're going to meet a man. Do you think I might be jealous? Is that where you're off to?'

'Yes,' she said, flooded with relief at this abrupt appearance of a lifebelt. 'Yes, that's it. Silly me to have been embarrassed, but you know me.' She gave a rather edgy laugh to which he didn't respond.

'And are you going to sleep with him? Forget I asked that.' He stood up and walked to the sink so that his back was towards her. 'If you want to bring him back here tonight, feel free. I won't be around.'

'Oh, sure, I'll think about it. Thanks.' She hovered for a while longer, wondering whether he had anything else to add, but he obviously hadn't, because he just stood there, staring out of the window.

Where was he going for the night? she wondered, frantic with jealousy, as she walked along the street towards the underground station.

Angela was no longer around. Had he found himself another sleeping partner already?

She tried to distract herself from the thought of that by thinking instead about the mystery of the non-existent company, but it didn't work.

She tried to remember every word of their short conversation, she tried to read clues behind what had been said and what hadn't, and the harder she tried, the more fuzzy her memory became.

The only two things she could remember with any clarity were his evasions when she had asked him whether he missed talking to her and had commented that her usefulness had now run its course.

Now another thought came to her. Did he see her as a threat to him? Did he think, as Angela had, that she was after a wedding ring and his money?

That unwelcome idea made her feel sick—she nearly

missed her stop, in fact—and it played uncomfortably on her mind as she walked towards the office block.

Chauffeur's daughter trying to better herself. Had she assumed that status in his eyes now? He had firsthand experience of how a woman could inveigle herself into bed with a man simply because she wanted his money. Look at Martha and his father. If ever he wanted an example of a gold-digger, he had no further to look than his own front doorstep.

She nearly missed the office block as well, and she had to backtrack on herself to get there.

But then, once she was inside the building, she felt her mind moving on to what was waiting for her and she ran up the stairs and let herself into her office, checking first to make sure that there were no nasty shocks in store for her, like Angela lurking around, which she wasn't.

In the smallest drawer in her desk, which she had cleared of its usual rubbish of paper-clips and rubber bands and now kept locked, Suzanne had been storing photocopies of everything she uncovered.

Now she set to work, and for a while Dane was forgotten.

Angela's office held the key to the riddle and she went there immediately, making sure beforehand that she checked every nook and cranny on the entire floor, including the stationery cupboard, to make sure that the nasty shock wasn't anywhere to be seen.

And, re-igniting her near-forgotten skill, learnt when she was thirteen at school from one of the boys in her class whose father made safes and could open locked ones just as easily, she clicked open the one locked drawer in Angela's desk with her credit card and set to work.

She took photocopies of everything. Later, alone, she would analyse it all. For the moment she just didn't want to get caught. But, glancing at some of the figures that she saw, neatly drawn into columns, she had a sickening feeling that things were far worse than she had imagined.

She worked quickly and noiselessly, her ears open for the slightest sound of a door opening, or the pad of footsteps along the corridor.

It was nearly seven o'clock by the time she returned to the apartment, and well after eleven before she finished reading and rereading all the documents that she had assiduously copied.

At midnight she heard Dane return. Hadn't he said that he was going to spend the night out? She frowned, pausing in her perusal of the papers spread on the bed, and then quickly gathered them up together and shoved them into the drawer of the bedside cabinet.

She didn't expect him to come into her room and when he did the first thing that flew into her head was, Thank God I've hidden the stuff. Then that instantaneous feeling was immediately replaced by surprised outrage. He hadn't even knocked! He had just pushed open the door as though he had every right in the world to invade her privacy, and was now standing there, darkly silhouetted in the doorframe.

'Yes?' she asked, sitting up on the bed and crossing her legs under her. Her nightshift left a great deal of thigh exposed, but there was nothing that she could do about that and she contented herself with a frosty expression. 'Do you want something or have you come into the wrong room?'

A dark flush crept along his cheekbones and for the first time that she could remember, ever, he looked ill at ease.

'You're still up,' he said flatly. His hand was still on the doorknob and he made no attempt actually to come inside the room.

'That's right. I'm still up.'

'What are you doing, sitting up in bed like that? Reading? I don't see a book anywhere.'

He was looking at her sharply but there was still something inexplicably awkward in his manner, which puzzled her.

'I wasn't reading a book,' she said coldly. She thought of the incriminating documents stuffed into the bedside drawer and flushed guiltily. Sooner or later she would have to tell him—in fact, sooner rather than later, but not now. She had to think first about what she had seen. Think very carefully and decide what move to make next.

'Then what are you doing?'

Was there no end to this man's arrogance? she wondered.

'Practising the ancient art of Transcendental Meditation,' she said scathingly. In the dark he was fairly forbidding standing there, looming. She wished that he would go away. 'Now, do you mind?'

'What's going on here? Why are you looking so secretive?'

Which immediately made her feel even more guilty. 'Nothing's going on and I'm not looking secretive. Have you been drinking by any chance?'

'Don't tell me that you're hiding a man in your closet?' His mouth twisted crookedly and underneath the cool sarcasm was something else, some other emotion which she couldn't quite put her finger on, as elusive as a wisp of smoke. What was he getting at?

'The bathroom, actually,' she said. 'The poor, shy fellow scurried off the minute he heard the front door slam. He thought, as I did, that you were going to be out for the night.'

There was a tight silence and she followed his eyes as they travelled away from the innocent closet to the innocent bathroom. He didn't really suspect that she was concealing a man in the bathroom, did he? The thought of that nearly made her burst out laughing.

She opened her mouth to tell him that it was a joke, for goodness' sake, but he didn't give her the time to utter a syllable. He stepped back and closed the bedroom door very quietly behind him and she heard his footsteps disappearing along the corridor back to his own quarters.

And Suzanne had too much on her mind to think further about that perplexing little interchange. She switched off the side-light and wondered what she was going to do now about those bits of paper lying in the bedside drawer.

There was, she thought with resignation, only one thing to do—only one thing that would tell her which way she should jump.

At five-thirty on Monday evening, when the office was beginning to clear of employees, she stopped Angela who was on her way out with her tan briefcase and asked if she could talk to her for a moment.

She had expected the relative silence of the place, now empty apart from a couple of managers who were working behind their closed doors further along the corridor, to be morally boosting, but now she wished that there were more noise around, more sounds to take her mind off what she had to do.

'What is it?' Angela's mouth turned down in irritation at the interruption to whatever plans she had made for the evening.

Suzanne looked at her, as she had looked at her for days, trying to trace some semblance of regret over her prematurely severed plans for her career, and now, as then, she could read nothing of the sort on the other woman's face.

'Unless it's important, whatever you have to say will simply have to wait until tomorrow morning.'

Her voice was icily off-putting, but Suzanne smiled pleasantly and said, 'I'm afraid it is rather important.'

'Five minutes.' Angela swept back along to her office, fully expecting Suzanne to follow her. 'Then I shall be leaving.'

Five minutes should do it, Suzanne thought, running back to fetch the file which she had found behind the cabinet, and which still carried only the original papers that had been there. Nothing had been added to it, nothing extracted.

If Angela scanned through the file and came up with something that could prove her innocence, if what was in there could be laughingly explained away, then Suzanne would let the matter drop and she would be more than happy to. She had decided from the start that she would let the other woman prove that there was nothing suspect about what had been discovered.

She shut the door behind her. 'I know you're busy,' she said without preliminaries and without sitting down, even though Angela had, behind her desk with its fax machine and computer and telephones—the desk of a woman on the up and up. 'However, I think you might be interested in seeing this.' She produced the file like a magician flourishing a bunch of flowers from a top hat. 'I found it a few days ago stuffed behind the filing cabinet in the office.'

'Why should I be interested in seeing that?'

'Because,' Suzanne explained, looking at the porcelain-like face intently, 'your handwriting is all over it. It appears to concern a company which doesn't exist. I know. I've checked it out.'

Angela didn't take the file. She stood up and walked over to the window and looked outside with her back to Suzanne. The lines of her body were rigid.

Now Suzanne realised that she had more than half hoped that this matter could be satisfactorily put to rest, that all her suspicions would be groundless, that an explanation would be provided. She watched the stiff back with dismay because none of these hopes was going to materialise.

'I also found other papers,' she said quietly, not mentioning where those other papers had been found. 'It appears that something is very wrong here and I think you know what I'm saying.'

Angela turned around and looked at her. She looked older, harder. Suzanne could see each line etched on that exquisite face; she could read the chilling admission on those narrowed lips.

'You have been a busy girl, haven't you?' Angela paused. 'Put that file on my desk and leave.'

'Of course.' Suzanne stepped forward, placed the file on the desk, and then said, in passing, 'I have photocopies of everything, naturally.'

They stared at each other like opponents at opposite sides of a boxing ring. The tension in the air was thick and Suzanne had a moment's light relief when she thought that if it came to a fist-fight, which she knew it never would, then Angela wouldn't stand a chance. There were, she thought, some advantages to being well-built.

'You were, I take it, prying behind locked doors?'

'I felt that the gravity of this warranted it.'

'I could have you sacked for that.'

'I don't think so,' Suzanne said, sounding far braver than she felt. 'You're working your notice; and anyway, there's no way that you could risk sacking me, knowing what I do.'

A muscle was working in Angela's jaw—a furious little tic that she couldn't control. Her long scarlet nails were digging into her arms.

'How much do you want?'

'What?' Suzanne looked at her in bewilderment.

'How much? For keeping your mouth shut.'

Suzanne backed towards the door. 'I don't want money. This needs to be sorted out between you and Dane. It's up to him what he does with you.' She looked at the other woman with dislike and horror. The palms of her hands felt clammy and she wiped them on her skirt, edging all the while to the door.

'In that case,' Angela said with a coldness that couldn't conceal the white fury underneath the tightly controlled surface, 'let me get one thing absolutely clear. I shall be out of here within a week. If you make the mistake of breathing a word of what you've found to anyone—anyone—then you have my word that your beloved Dane will pay the price.'

'What do you mean?'

'There's only one thing that he wants,' Angela said, smiling without humour, 'and I shall make damn sure that he doesn't get it if you tell him about this.'

'What thing?' She tried to insert some bravado into her voice and failed.

'Didn't he tell you? You do surprise me. And I thought that the two of you were inseparable.' There was an ugly twist to her lips as she said that. 'He doesn't want *you*, my dear, just like he never wanted *me*. The only thing Dane Sutherland wants is his father's company and revenge on that stepmother of his.' She saw the shocked expression on Suzanne's face and smiled. 'Why do you think he returned when he did? Because the foundations for the takeover of Martha's company are almost complete.'

'He told you this?' Suzanne whispered. Her hands felt clammy again.

'Hardly. Dane only reveals what he wants to, as you must have discovered by now, my dear. No, when I worked for him in New York, I had access to his files. A couple of opportune calls alerted me to one particular

file and I did a few rudimentary checks and discovered
it all by myself—information which I intended to keep
to myself, or else store for a rainy day. The rainy day
has arrived, unfortunately. Dane made it quite clear that
he never wanted me—' the beautiful face contorted with
the rage of a woman spurned '—and now I have the
wherewithal to destroy the one thing he prizes most
highly.

'The point is this: you expose me and you will also
risk destroying everything he's worked towards for the
past three years. If you do, then he will never forgive
you, and where—' she smiled again—the same reptilian
smile that carried an element of menace behind it
'—would that leave you and your silly love? Not that
you stand a chance of marrying the man. Oh, no. But
do you want him to hate you?' The question dangled
provocatively in the air. 'I hope we understand one another.'

Suzanne neither confirmed or denied that one. She had
finally reached the door and she opened it and let herself
out, then she fled down the corridor and down the flights
of stairs, ignoring the lift, just in case she found herself
confined in there with Angela.

Her mind was reeling from an overload of information. Outside, in the open air, she still felt trapped and
suffocating. The choice was simple: let Angela get away
with fraud or else ruin Dane's stealthy takeover of his
father's company.

She made her way back to the apartment, let herself
in, prepared her meal, which she couldn't eat because it
tasted like cotton wool, and then waited for Dane to get
back.

It was after eleven when the front door slammed. She
had had time to have a bath, change into her jeans and
shirt, time to think about how she was going to handle
this. She sprang to her feet and confronted him as he
was about to head off towards his bedroom.

'Yes?' he enquired coolly, taking her in with one sweeping glance.

'I have to talk to you.'

'Not now.' He prepared to move on and she sprinted towards him and circled his wrist with her fingers.

'Please,' she said stubbornly, 'it's important.'

Dane looked at her face, then at the slender fingers curved around his wrist, then back at her face. He shrugged and she led him into the sitting room and then began pacing the floor until he snapped impatiently, 'Will you sit down? I'm getting seasick looking at you walking up and down like that.'

Suzanne sat down, leaning towards him with her elbows on her knees, and he crossed his legs, his ankle resting on his knee.

'Now what do you want to talk to me about?' he drawled in a vaguely bored manner. To cap it all, he yawned.

'If you could struggle to keep yourself awake,' Suzanne said acidly, 'you might be very interested to hear about what I've got to say.' He responded to that statement with a marked lack of interest.

'There's an off chance of that, I suppose.'

'I'm not sure where to begin,' she said, ignoring his tone of voice. She stood up, began pacing once again, then sat back down and said sarcastically, 'Sorry, I forgot that my walking about makes you seasick. We can't have you seasick and racked with tiredness, can we?' She frowned slightly. 'The fact is that I've been working rather hard at the office.'

'If it's about a pay rise, then you'll have to discuss that with your boss. I should wait until Angela leaves, though. I don't think that you'll find her very obliging in that respect.'

He began to stand up and she said quickly, 'Nothing to do with a pay rise. It's about Angela, actually.'

There was silence and he sat back down, only now there was nothing sleepy or bored in his expression.

'What about her?'

'I've been doing a lot of overtime,' Suzanne said, moving on quickly so that she didn't lose his attention, 'digging into a lot of files, mostly out of curiosity, and also using them as sort of test cases to see whether I would have handled the account in the same way.'

'And…?'

'And I came across a file, quite by accident. It had been shoved behind the filing cabinet. One of Angela's files, as a matter of fact, with no input by anyone else. All her handwriting—just a few scribbles and notes and mention of a company which I discovered doesn't exist.'

'I see.' There was a deadly calm in his voice.

'She's been embezzling money, Dane. I'm sorry. I have other documentary proof which I've photocopied. It hasn't been going on for very long but the amounts of money involved have been increasing steadily.'

'I see.'

'I can fetch all the stuff for you,' she said, standing up.

He looked at her and said in the same chilling voice, 'Is there anything else?'

'Yes.' She hesitated, then blurted out, 'She told me that if I went to you with this then she would make sure that your plans to take over your father's company were destroyed.'

'She told you that, did she?' His face darkened and he stood up suddenly.

'Apparently she uncovered some of it by accident and then dug around until she found the proof she needed to confirm it.'

'I see.' The calm, the stillness was more frightening than an explosion of anger. 'Thank you for coming to me,' he said, his thoughts somewhere else, then he looked at her for a long while.

'Tomorrow,' he said, 'we're going on a little trip. The time has come to go back home.'

CHAPTER NINE

THEY ended up leaving shortly after lunch, with the sun pouring down out of a blue sky. Not the sort of day for confrontations, but there would be one. Suzanne could sense it. The current quiet was like the eye of a hurricane slowly shifting position, presaging a storm ahead.

Dane didn't go to work in the morning. Suzanne got up early, at seven-thirty, to find him on the phone, his voice low and rapid, with a stack of papers in front of him. He glanced up as she entered but he didn't seem to see her at all, and almost immediately he returned to his conversation and she left the sitting room, quietly shutting the door behind her.

She had had time to think about what was going on, time to piece together his abrupt departure to America, his return to England, his knowledge of what had been happening to his father's company, which at the time had struck her as peculiar but not now. He had *needed* to know, as he'd waited on the sidelines—watched and waited, and prepared his trap.

She made a half-hearted attempt at breakfast, made them both cups of coffee and strolled in to find him still heavily involved on the telephone. He waved for her to put the coffee on the table and she left the room again, feeling a bit like a waitress, someone to be seen and heard only when necessary.

He didn't emerge until a little after eleven and she

immediately asked, without beating about the bush, 'What exactly is going to happen?'

'Thanks for the cup of coffee.' He strolled over to the kitchen table, sat down and ran his fingers through his dark hair in a weary gesture.

'You haven't answered my question.'

'You are an extremely persistent creature,' he told her, looking at her.

'It takes one, I suppose, to know one.' She sat down opposite him. 'You look half-dead. How long have you been up?' She sipped some of her coffee, her fourth cup of the day, because she couldn't seem to get her mind round anything at all and drinking cups of coffee gave her something to do. It also steadied her nerves. There had been a time, she thought, when chocolate would have been the only substitute, and that time seemed like a million light years away.

'Since five,' he answered, rubbing his eyes with his fingers.

'On the telephone?'

'That's right. Waking people up and getting them to work for their money.'

'I'm sure they all appreciated that,' she answered with a smile. It felt quite unreal to be sitting here, talking to him, when she should have been at work. It was a relief not to have to face Angela after the accusations of the night before, that much was true.

'Right.' He stood up and absent-mindedly tucked his shirt back into the waistband of his trousers. 'Are you ready?'

'I've been meaning to ask,' Suzanne said awkwardly, 'whether it's absolutely essential for me to come. This is all to do with you, plans you made a long time ago. Do you really want me tagging along?'

'I'm giving you the chance of a lifetime,' he said with a lazy smile which wasn't directed at her, she knew, but at some thought flitting through his head. 'I'm taking you back to the source of your bitterness. Don't you want that? Don't you want to see Martha and have the opportunity to give vent to the anger which you've misdirected at me all these months?'

See Martha. The thought of that made her go a little shaky at the knees. She had never actually confronted Martha with any of her bitter grievances. At the time of her father's death she had been too confused and lost to think, and afterwards she had moved to London and thoughts of Martha had been little more than fantasies which conspired to make her life hell, and which she had never thought of putting to rest by paying the woman a visit.

'I suppose so,' she said doubtfully, and he laughed— a hard, humourless sound that made her feel even more nervous.

'You suppose so? Is that the best you can do?'

'What would be the point of throwing recriminations at her?' she asked. 'She'll just deny everything anyway. She'll just tell me that my father could have left any time he wanted to, that it was necessary to get rid of those workers, that she's looked after the house and grounds to the best of her ability. And I shall just get tongue-tied and inarticulate with rage because she'll be patting that dyed blonde hair of hers and looking at her painted fingernails and wondering how she can shift me out of her house.'

'My house,' Dane corrected her.

'Yes, I know, but she's been there for three years and you never once went back. She must consider that she has right of ownership now.'

'Then she'll be making a big mistake.' He consulted his watch and then said, 'Time to go.' At which Suzanne sprang to her feet and gave him a weak smile of agreement.

'No need to look as though you're about to be delivered to the sharks,' he told her on the way down to the car. 'It's a bright, sunny day and you're not at work.'

'No, work might have been a little awkward with Angela after yesterday.'

He laughed and looked at her sideways. 'What mastery of understatement.' He opened the passenger door for her, slammed it once she was sitting and then let himself into the driver's seat.

'When did you decide to…?' The words fizzled out as the car moved smoothly out of the courtyard and into the congested streets of London.

'To repay Martha for fleecing my father?'

'He was happy.'

'She used him, and what goes around comes around.'

His expression was unforgiving and she looked out of the window. Had Angela been right? Was every ounce of his considerable personality devoted to this one thing so that there was nothing left over for anything or anyone else? She didn't like to think along those lines because that would be to deny any camaraderie between them, to admit that she had been nothing to him—nothing at all.

She closed her eyes and rested her head against the back of the seat and sighed. 'I could get used to this,' she murmured.

'To what? Being driven in a BMW or being driven by me in a BMW?' He laughed under his breath and she shot him a look from under her lashes. Why did he have to ask sexy questions like that, she wondered, when he must know how much they disturbed her equilibrium?

'Public transport can be a bit of a headache,' she told him blandly. 'All those bodies and the smell of stale sweat.'

'Charming. Why don't you get a taxi to work in that case?'

'And why don't I fly to Mars for my next holiday?'

He laughed, relaxed and they drove for a while in companionable silence. London was packed with people and cars. Suzanne watched them idly and wondered whether she would miss it if she decided to go back to the Midlands to live. She had been desperate to leave at the time, but now she seemed to have come to terms with her father's death and with the fact that her own life had to go on, and returning to the peace of her home town wasn't the same frightful proposition that it had been even a few weeks ago.

'Talk to me,' he said suddenly from next to her, and she opened her eyes reluctantly.

'What about?'

'Anything. I like the sound of your voice.'

She felt a flush of pleasure rush through her. 'We could discuss Angela,' she began, and he frowned.

'Talk to me about anything but work.'

'I think I might go back home to live,' she said eventually, and the flush of pleasure died as soon as she saw him nod in agreement.

'That's a good idea. I knew you would eventually.'

'Thank you very much,' she said coolly. 'Do I detect a note of relief there?'

'Why are you nettled because I intimated that it would be a good idea for you to go back to the country?' There was a small smile playing on the corners of his mouth.

'Because I can feel one of your speeches coming on. About how I never really was cut out for London, that I belong in the country where the pace is slow enough for a dimwit like me to cope.'

'You weren't exactly a dimwit when you exposed Angela,' Dane contradicted her smoothly, and it didn't escape her that he had successfully manoeuvred his way around her question. They were now out of London and

on the motorway, which was similarly clogged with traffic.

'I would never have suspected a thing if I hadn't
found that folder stuffed behind the filing cabinet.'

'But you did, and you worked away at it until you
found out what was going on.'

'I know. I'm a genius.'

'What a loss to that company when you left to move
to London.'

'Indeed. I'm sure they're still weeping and wailing
and wringing their hands over it.'

'Will you go back there to work?' he asked conversationally.

So now, she thought, he was assuming that she had
already made up her mind to move back. He couldn't
wait to get rid of her.

'No,' she said abruptly. 'It's too small.'

'Thought you'd say that.'

'I wish you wouldn't act as though you know everything about me,' she muttered crossly. 'Why do you
bother to ask questions if you already know the answers?'

'Are you hungry?' he asked, and she scowled at his
profile. He certainly had simmered down since this
morning, she thought. He looked like a man, in fact,
without a care in the world. Or maybe he only looked
like that because he knew that he was going to be rid of
her shortly. Was that what had put him in this jaunty
mood? That and the fact that the inevitable was now
going to become the inescapable?

'No.'

'We'll stop at one of the service stations. Sausage,
beans and chips.'

'Yummy,' Suzanne said sulkily, and he ignored her.

The service station was crowded and in the end they
had two hamburgers in the car with two cans of drink

precariously propped on the dashboard. She ate her food with vigour, licking her fingers afterwards, and when Dane gave her his opinions on the quality of the meat in the hamburger she rapidly pointed out, in as lofty a voice as she could manage because she was still irked at the speed with which he wanted to dispatch her out of his apartment and back to the dubious thrills of the countryside, that he would grow into an old, cantankerous, know-it-all, predictable bore.

'Good.' He laughed loudly. 'I shall look forward to that.'

'Why are you in such a good mood, anyway?' she asked tartly, after he had disposed of the debris and returned to the car. 'Shouldn't you,' she persisted like a dog with a bone, 'be tense and nervous? You were this morning.'

He eased his car back onto the motorway and into the fast lane, overtaking everything in front of him. Suzanne looked at the long fingers deftly manipulating the gear stick, at the faint smile on his lips, and felt like hitting him.

'Well?' she demanded, and he looked at her briefly, then back at the road.

'I'm in a good mood, darling, because everything is beginning to fall into place. The chase is almost over and the quarry is now in sight.'

'How nice that you can see into the future, make the right moves and end up exactly where you want to be.'

It was a far cry from her, she thought, who couldn't see further than her nose—or else she would never have fallen in love with him—had no long-range plans, and was buoyed along on the vague hope that everything would turn out all right.

'It is, isn't it?' They were cruising steadily in the inside lane now, and the car was eating up the miles. Soon they would be there, back at the grand house which held such bitter memories for her, back at the cottage which had probably been remodelled into a gaudy, tacky self-contained unit for when there were too many guests for the main house.

'There's no need to sound so smug about it. Smugness isn't a very pleasant trait.'

'But, according to you, I haven't got any pleasant traits,' he pointed out. He paused and said in a voice that sounded surprised, 'So why have you fallen in love with me?'

Suzanne looked at him with stiff-faced shock, then she felt as though her blood had turned to fire and was burning a path through her from the inside.

'You're crazy,' she whispered. She wanted to look outside at the passing traffic, but she felt compelled to look at his face, to try and glean something from that amused, satisfied expression.

'Am I? There was no man in your room the other night, was there, Suzie?' he asked softly, and when she didn't reply he prompted again, 'Well? Was there?'

'I never said that there was. You did.'

'Ah, but you didn't deny it. Why not? Did you want to make me jealous?'

'Don't be ridiculous.'

'You were reading all those papers about the company that Angela fabricated so that she could defraud my company. When I came in, you stuffed them somewhere out of sight and that was the reason that you looked so guilty.'

Suzanne could hardly hear him. There was a buzz in her ears and her joints seemed to have solidified. If she had been the fainting sort, then she would have fainted, but since she was not delicate enough for such theatrical responses she contented herself with staring blindly ahead of her.

'I knew for a while that you found me attractive,' he

continued, when she would have rather that he had shut up, 'but I've only now put two and two together.'

'I am not in love with you. And I don't want to be listening to this.'

'Of course you're in love with me.'

'If you want to think that, then go right ahead. Who am I to stop you?'

He began to whistle under his breath and it dawned on her that the reason why he was so light-hearted about the whole thing was that he now thought that he had her where he wanted her. In the palm of his hand. He hadn't forgiven her for turning him out of her bedroom and now he would have her. His male pride would be restored. She felt tears of anger and humiliation prick her eyes and she dragged her attention away from his face and to the road.

They had left the motorway and were driving along back roads—country roads surrounded mostly by open fields full of sheep and cows. In the sharp sunlight, the greens looked iridescent and the sky was a clear, untainted blue.

'I shall never sleep with you,' she said in a low, shaky voice. 'Never!'

'So you admit that what I've said is true.'

He stopped the car in a lay-by and Suzanne watched him apprehensively, feeling like a trapped rabbit.

'I'll get over it,' she said in a strangled voice. She didn't know whether she hated that gleaming look in his eyes—like that of a bird of prey contemplating its next kill—more than she would have hated long sermons about how he'd never meant to hurt her. She couldn't imagine Dane Sutherland giving long sermons of remorse about not having wanted to hurt or offend, so at least that horrifying prospect was ruled out.

'Why have we stopped here?'

'Because we're very nearly at the house and we might as well talk while we can.'

'There's nothing to talk about,' she muttered bitterly. 'I suppose you're well and truly satisfied? Why couldn't you have left me where I was?' The words were wrenched out of her and she still wasn't looking at him.

'You were miserable.'

'I was happy to be miserable!' She would have eventually coped with that kind of misery, but this kind of misery was beyond her.

'I still want you,' he said in a matter-of-fact kind of voice, although she could feel his eyes burning into her. One hand was on the gear stick, his other rested lightly on the driving wheel, and no one seeing them from a distance could have guessed that they were having this urgent, surreal conversation. 'It galls me to think that I do, but there it is.'

'I don't want to hear about want! You're like a fisherman intrigued by the one that got away! Why can't you take yourself off to another bed and another woman? There must be hundreds out there who would climb into bed with you before you'd even finished asking the question.'

'But none of them provide the challenge that you do.'

'Is that why you dragged me up here?' she flung at him. 'Because you thought that you might catch me with my guard down, vulnerable back on home territory? Did you think that you could take me before I left London once and for all?'

'I'm not a complete monster.' He sounded so calm and controlled. She, on the other hand, knew that she was beginning to border on the hysterical and she resented him bitterly for exposing her vulnerability.

'Aren't you?'

'You've come to terms with your father's death.'

'And for that you magnanimously take all the credit?'

'Of course I don't, but I did give you a purpose in your life.'

'A million thanks,' she said sarcastically. 'You're obviously in the wrong profession. You should be out there on the world stage, working toward universal peace.'

He laughed drily and his eyes, when they rested on her, were warm and lazy; she turned away abruptly and stared straight ahead.

'You're very amusing, do you know that?'

'I think you've mentioned that before.' While she stared, white-faced, through the window, her fingers fidgeted nervously together on her lap.

'And desirable.' The word hung provocatively in the air, just, she realised, as he meant it to, conjuring up all sorts of images and emotions with which he no doubt hoped to undermine her resolution. He didn't lay a finger on her, though, and that was the cleverest ploy of all. To hear him speak like that without touching was like being sucked into somewhere dark and soft and inviting. She had to grit her teeth together to fight the temptation to look at him and give in.

'Think about it,' he said softly, and then started up the engine, which purred into life like a big beast ready to run.

She thought about it. In fact, it was all she thought about for the remainder of the journey and she only found her thoughts moving along when the car swung up the familiar tree-lined avenue, with its fields stretching placidly away as far as the eye could see, and turned into the drive that led towards the house.

'Is Martha expecting us?'

'No.' His expression was grim but there was a sense of anticipation about him that gave him a sort of restless energy which she could feel rather than see on his face. 'But she'll be there.'

'How do you know?'

'I have arranged it.'

They passed the cottage on their left as they drove slowly up, and Suzanne's eyes lingered hungrily on it. It looked the same. Small, red-bricked, with small windows and ivy creeping up the front. Her father had fought an amicable battle with the ivy to prevent it from taking over, and presumably the gardener now did that little duty.

Thoughts and memories of her father which had lain dormant resurfaced in confusing profusion like snippets of films disjointedly thrown together and played back at high speed.

Brief images of childhood—holding her father's hand and going for walks, listening to him explain to her about the different types of flowers in the fields and the different types of birds that swooped down for bread thrown out by them religiously every morning. Visions of adolescence—her first grown-up dress awkwardly presented to her by her father on her thirteenth birthday. She half expected to see him walk out of the front door and wave at them, but, of course, he didn't.

'Are you all right?' Dane asked from beside her, and she leant her head against the window-pane.

'I'm fine,' she answered a little shortly. The cottage was lost from sight and within a couple of minutes the vast house appeared in front of them, like a familiar friend not seen for a long time. She seemed to remember every brick and every angle of every window, and she wondered whether it was the same for him too. After all, it was a long time since he had last laid eyes on it.

She looked at him sideways, from under her lashes. 'Does it feel like coming home to you?' she asked hesitantly, and he didn't look at her when he replied.

'Oh, yes,' he murmured, his eyes on the house—his house. 'Everywhere else has simply been in transit. This

is the destination that's waited for me from the very first
day I left.'

There were no cars in the courtyard and for a second
she wondered whether the trip would result in the anti-
climax of finding no one in, but she remembered the
second courtyard behind the house, by the stables, and
realised that that was where the cars would be parked.

Martha had always insisted on having two cars: the
Rolls-Royce—a silvery blue one which Suzanne's father
had used to drive her from one appointment to another—
and her convertible Mercedes sports car which she drove
herself when she didn't want to be chauffeured. Suzanne
could remember seeing the burgundy car flash past in
summer, with the roof down and Martha behind the
wheel, her blonde hair neatly contained under a silk
scarf, looking like a movie star.

She felt a lump of resentment at the back of her throat
and for the first time was profoundly glad that Dane had
asked her along on this trip.

A youngish girl answered the door when they rang.
Suzanne had never seen her before. Enid, who had been
the housemaid there for years, had been summarily des-
patched when old Mr Sutherland had died. Martha had
never liked her; she had felt that the old woman under-
mined her authority, and she had taken the first available
opportunity to get rid of her, after which there had been
a succession of maids because none of them ever seemed
to last the course. Martha, Suzanne recalled, had a way
of issuing orders that would try the most patient of souls.

This girl was plump, with dark hair tied back in a
pony-tail, and she looked at Dane with surreptitious interest but no recognition.

'Mrs Sutherland is in the drawing room,' she said. 'If
you'd like to follow me…?'

'I know the way,' Dane said, which startled her somewhat, but she had obviously been trained to listen to

commands, because she obediently fell back and shut the door behind them.

'I see that Martha has imposed her own tastes on the place,' Dane said, looking around him once the housemaid had retired to the kitchen. His face was disapproving and Suzanne followed his eyes. She had become accustomed to the decor, all changed after old Mr Sutherland's death, but she could appreciate how strange it must seem to Dane.

Where there had once been paint, there was now wallpaper in the large hallway, busily patterned with flowers, more suited to a bedroom than to the high-ceilinged hall, which seemed to lose its dignity under the bombardment of roses climbing vines with the odd bird peeping out from behind the leaves.

'She said that the original paintwork was too fusty.'

'Not what she said when she first came here with my father,' Dane muttered grimly. 'She was falling over herself with delight then.'

Suzanne didn't say anything, and they both lapsed into silence as they walked towards the drawing room.

Martha was waiting for them. She stood up as they came in, not looking a day older than when Suzanne had last seen her. She was wearing a canary-yellow suit with a strand of pearls around her neck and an expression of stunned surprise on her face.

'Dane, darling,' she said, recovering quickly. 'I'm afraid I wasn't expecting you. I thought—well, that Mr Martin…'

'Couldn't make it,' Dane said smoothly, stepping away from the outstretched arms. 'I'm here instead.'

'Of course. Do sit. It's lovely to see you.' She had, Suzanne noticed, pretended not to have noticed her presence at all.

'You remember Suzanne Stanton, don't you, Martha?'

Dane asked, and Martha reluctantly looked at her with a marked change of expression.

'Of course. I was tremendously sorry about your father.'

'I doubt that,' Suzanne said politely, and the atmosphere shifted. Now there were no overtones of cordiality.

'What are you doing here, anyway?' she asked curtly.

'She's with me,' Dane said coldly. 'I asked her to come.'

'Really? How cosy.' She looked away from Suzanne, as though the sight of her aroused too much distaste, and resumed her seat on the sofa, which put her at an immediate disadvantage since neither Suzanne nor Dane sat down.

'But, of course, I know all about your affair with the girl,' Martha said, and now that the mask of genial hostess had dropped it wasn't difficult to see the tight-mouthed dislike on the attractive face, with its fine lines peeping through the camouflage of foundation and make-up. Martha was beginning to look her age, but she would never be one to concede gracefully. The yellow skirt was still a goodish way above the knees and her make-up was still heavily applied.

'How common of you, Dane, darling. I would have thought that you might have known better.'

There was a deep silence, and there was such cold dislike on Dane's face that Martha was forced to look away.

'It would be nice if you didn't discuss me as though I wasn't present,' Suzanne said, with a white rage of her own burning inside her and threatening to explode. 'If you wish to hurl insults at my expense, then do please show enough good breeding to do it to my face.' The breeding bit, Suzanne knew, would hit home, and it did. Martha's face contorted with fury.

'Fine. In that case, I don't understand what my step-son is doing consorting with a tramp like you. I've heard all about what's going on, and if your father—' she glanced at Dane '—knew what had been going on he would turn in his grave.'

'And where does your information come from?' Dane asked with chilling politeness. 'Or need I ask?'

Martha laughed, just as there was a knock on the door. There was something quite ugly in that laugh. 'On cue,' she said by way of response. 'As you're as uninterested in catching up with old times as I am, Dane, then I might as well get straight to the point. Your trip here has been a waste of time. I know why you've come and you've made a mistake. For once in your life, you've got it wrong.' There was intense hatred in those eyes and Suzanne looked at Dane and Martha and wondered what else lay beneath this act being played out between them.

The door opened, and all three heads swung round. It struck her that the scenario was in a way highly theatrical, but with an element of danger running through it that made it real.

Dane's expression hardly altered at all. It was as though he had been half expecting the intrusion, but Suzanne's mouth fell open with shock as Angela walked in, besuited like Martha but in darker colours, vibrantly attractive but with the allure of a deadly snake.

'I wondered when you would come up here,' she said conversationally, moving to sit next to Martha, where the physical similarities between them were even more noticeable. Both small, both blonde. With the right age-gap, they could have passed for mother and daughter, but, as it was, they looked like two sisters made from the same mould. Or maybe it was the similarity of expression that lent them that curious resemblance. A sort of triumphant, distasteful glee.

'I did warn you,' Angela said, looking at Suzanne,

'but of course you had to do it your way, and now you've ruined poor Dane's plans.

'I would have left with some money—some highly deserved money,' she said in a vicious voice to Dane, 'but then your prying little lover discovered everything, so what else could I possibly do...?'

'There's another buyer,' Martha said with open gloating in her voice. 'I've been having urgent talks to Geoffrey Martin and Greg Thompson, and you've wasted your time. The company has already been sold.'

Suzanne couldn't look at him. Was Martha right? *Had* he come so far to lose it all like sand between his fingers? Had she blown it? She felt sick. She realised that she loved him so much that it hardly mattered whether she meant nothing to him; she just wanted this one moment not to collapse, least of all because of her.

Dane walked across the patio doors and stared out without a flicker of emotion on his dark face.

'You should never,' Angela told him with malevolent dislike, 'have involved yourself with that girl. If you hadn't, none of this would have happened.'

He turned to face them and his personality was such that they all stared at him with varying degrees of fascination.

'Did you really think that you could outsmart me, Angela?'

The words fell into the silence like a stone thrown into a pond, creating ever widening ripples that manifested themselves in growing looks of doubt and horror on the faces of Angela and Martha.

'The directors of the company—'

'Have been working on my behalf,' he finished for Martha. 'They have been in communication with me from the very day that I left England. Your company, my dear, no longer belongs to you.'

Martha half rose and her face blanched. 'I have been

assured...' she began faintly, falling back down onto the sofa.

'Every move you have made has been relayed to me. You haven't breathed without me knowing it from thousands of miles away.' He walked towards the centre of the room. 'The deal was done and completed last night,' he told his intent audience.

'As for you,' he said to Angela, 'you will repay every cent that you've embezzled if you have to clean floors to do it, because, as I stand here, I can promise you that you will find it extremely difficult to get a job of any standing anywhere in America, or here for that matter. Most companies do not appreciate employees who work against their bosses, when they think that it suits them.'

'You can't do that,' she said in a choking voice, and he didn't even have to reply because his answer to that was written on his face.

He crooked a finger in the direction of Suzanne, who had been hanging onto this exchange, hardly daring to breathe. Now she walked slowly towards him and to her intense surprise he slung his arm around her shoulder.

'You may have forgotten, Martha,' he said in a voice as smooth and as sharp as a knife, 'but this house belongs to me. I want you and your belongings out of it by the end of today.'

'But where will I go?' she demanded, and her exquisitely made-up face was contorted with horror. Both she and Angela looked as though the world had collapsed around their ears.

'You must still have some money from my father's legacy. Use it. You can take the cars. Sell them if you have to.' But my mind is made up, his voice said. 'Suzanne will make sure that you leave on time.'

He looked at her; she felt his head turn and his eyes

rest on her for a moment, and when he next spoke his voice was softer. 'She has every reason to want you out of here, and she has every right, because I intend to marry her.'

CHAPTER TEN

IT WAS a goodish while before Suzanne could ask Dane about that extraordinary statement.

Things, after he had spoken, moved swiftly and with momentum, like a cart sent spinning down a hill, gathering speed.

She hadn't known whether he had really expected her to assist Martha with her departure, but he obviously had, because now he left them both in the room and headed towards the study where, he said, he had some things to sort out.

One of those things appeared to be Angela, who followed him in a state of panic, her high voice disappearing down the corridor in a series of semi-wails and argumentative fury. If Dane paid the slightest bit of notice to this pleading, then it certainly wasn't immediately apparent, because his deep voice was conspicuous by its absence.

Suzanne, however much bitterness was stored up, could feel herself beginning to have twinges of sympathy for Martha, but any such sympathy was killed virtually before it began because Martha was not about to become sweetness and light now that she had been forced out of her castle.

'I suppose you can't wait to start gloating,' she said, and her face was still a mask of fury—the fury of someone summarily stripped of her honour. She didn't give Suzanne an opportunity to answer that, and for the rest of the day, as she collected her belongings, she continued a vicious monologue of insults and innuendo.

After a while, Suzanne became completely impervious, and she followed Martha through the vast rooms, half-heartedly making sure that everything was collected, but thinking deeply about what Dane had said.

Had he meant it? Had that been a proposal of marriage out there? A real proposal of marriage? Or had it been a carefully calculated statement designed to work in his favour and arouse maximum reaction from two people who had had the temerity to think that they could outsmart him?

She frowned as she went from room to room, looking up when Martha said something outrageous and then returning to her quiet speculation.

Which, of course, only served to infuriate Martha further. She threw her expensive clothes into her equally expensive suitcases, and when Suzanne remarked mildly that she would have a hell of a job getting the creases out she gave vent to five minutes of undiluted rage, which included everything from Dane to his father, to Suzanne, to her father, to the awful nightmare of living in a backward village miles away from any good shops.

Before she was even halfway through the tirade, Suzanne was lost in speculation once again, this time trying to decipher the tone of Dane's voice when he had uttered those words. She hadn't been looking at him, so she had no idea what his expression had been, and her imagination busily tried to fill in the missing pieces, which left her with a slight headache.

Martha had packed as much as she possibly could by early evening. She had stripped the house of everything which she claimed belonged to her, and various things which Suzanne suspected didn't and which she would casually mention to Dane some time later on.

Martha had eyed several of the paintings on the walls

with a proprietorial gleam in her eyes, and at that Suzanne had quietly insisted that she talk to Dane, since the paintings had been in the Sutherland family for generations and belonged to the house, which had been when Martha had ungraciously conceded defeat.

Now she stood there in the hallway, surrounded by at least a dozen Louis Vuitton bags of various sizes, and it was a relief when Dane appeared from the direction of the study, because Suzanne had no idea what she was supposed to do next.

'All done, Martha?' he asked with a studied politeness that made his stepmother's face tighten. He put his arm over Suzanne's shoulders, the way he had done earlier on in the drawing room, and she began frantically speculating all over again.

'I hope that you carry this on your conscience for the rest of your life,' Martha told him with icy hatred.

Angela was nowhere to be seen. Had she been dismissed earlier on by Dane? Suzanne wondered.

'In the same way that you no doubt carry the burden of those dismissed workers on your conscience?' he replied with barely concealed distaste. 'You at least have the wherewithal to carry on until you find yourself another wealthy man.'

Martha's eyes were flicking between the two of them.

'I can't say that I wish you both happiness,' she said with a little shrug. 'I don't care enough whether you make a go of your marriage or not.' She directed her cold blue eyes in Suzanne's direction. 'I dare say you worked hard enough to get him, my dear, but you'll never keep him, you know. You're far too gauche and plain.'

She glanced at Dane and this time there was a different look in her eyes—one which Suzanne couldn't interpret. 'It could have been different between us, Dane,' she said, and Suzanne wondered whether she could hear something throaty in that voice or whether her imagination was playing tricks on her.

'I don't think so, Martha,' he drawled, and his arm tightened on Suzanne's shoulder. Perceptibly. 'Now, I really think that it's time we brought these pleasantries to an end, don't you? Harris is waiting to take you in the Rolls. The rest of your belongings will be forwarded to whatever your new address is.'

'America.' Martha looked at him, challenging him to question that remark, and when he didn't she said, with clipped irritation because no curiosity had been evoked, 'Angela and I have decided to go into business together. We intend to set up an interior design company. Angela says that there's immense scope in the States for my kind of taste in decor.'

Suzanne lowered her head and choked back a laugh at that, although the pair of them would probably make a roaring success of it. They were both forceful enough to browbeat any potential clients into terrified submission.

'Now,' Dane said softly, turning to Suzanne as soon as Martha and her bags had departed. 'You.' He held her at arm's length, with his hands on her shoulders, and she looked up at him nervously, not quite knowing what the next scene in this remarkable play was going to be.

'Me,' she said numbly, looking away, and he tilted her head back to him. There was a slight smile on his lips.

'There is, I believe, some unfinished business between us.'

Her heart gave a leap.

'Dane...' she began, and he put his fingers on her lips.

'Don't tell me that you're going to argue with your husband-to-be,' he murmured, his eyes dark, and this time she felt as though everything inside her had undergone a scramble.

'You didn't mean that.'

'Didn't I?' he asked huskily.

'You said it for effect.'

'Is that so?' He led her out of the hall, up the grand staircase which had aroused such open-mouthed awe in her ever since she had been a child, along the corridor, hung on either side with daunting portraits of his various ancestors, and pushed open the door at the far end. The door to his bedroom.

This room, at least, had not suffered under the hands of Martha. Whilst most of the other rooms had been decorated in various floral patterns, this one was starkly masculine. The walls were blue—a vibrant blue which should have looked hideous but in fact looked rich and inviting. The bedroom furniture was of dark wood and the huge bay windows looked out over the extensive gardens and fields.

Suzanne, her fingers still linked with his, fell back at the doorway.

'My bedroom,' he said unnecessarily, turning to her. He stroked the side of her face and, where he touched, her skin tingled.

'You really want to marry me?' she asked, and he laughed under his breath.

'You make it sound as though I'm letting myself in for something horrendous.' His voice was like a caress. She couldn't think straight when he spoke like that.

'You mean that you'd marry me just because you want to sleep with me?' she asked in a high voice.

'Would that be so shocking?'

She felt her body, which had been floating somewhere in the clouds, plummet back to earth with a bang.

'Yes. Yes, it would.' She tried to tug her hand out of his and he kept it firmly clasped between his fingers.

'In that case,' he said, moving towards her and tangling his fingers in her long hair, 'what about if I told you that I intend to marry you because I've fallen madly in love with you. Would that do?'

'You've fallen in love with me?'

'There you go. Repeating everything I say. A very bad habit.'

'Please, Dane,' she whispered, 'don't tease.'

'Tease? Oh, my darling.' He kissed her, gently, then with growing force, his tongue exploring her mouth, and she groaned. 'I've never been more serious in my life. Years ago, when we first knew one another, I thought you an interesting little thing. How was I to know that you'd mature into a witch and place this irrational spell on me?'

She wrapped her arms around his neck. He loved her! Her head was singing and everything inside seemed to have taken glorious flight.

He lifted her off her feet and placed her in the centre of his king-size bed, then he lay down beside her, propped up on one elbow so that he could look at her.

'I don't know when I first realised that I was attracted to you. I think that something inside me stirred the very first time I laid eyes on you in that deplorable bedsit of yours. I hadn't gone intending to bring you back with me, but I knew there and then that I had to. I tried to tell myself that it was all purely altruistic, but I found myself thinking about you more and more, and whenever I was with you my eyes kept straying and my thoughts followed suit.'

'But I was fat!' Suzanne said happily. What she really wanted to say was that she had felt exactly the same way, but she wanted him to carry on talking, too.

'Don't ever think that your size doesn't make you intensely attractive,' he murmured, unbuttoning her blouse and slipping his hand into her bra to scoop out her full breast. She obligingly unfastened it at the front and he groaned.

'When you walked in on that wretched party dressed in next to nothing and all those men couldn't take their eyes off you, I felt that I was going mad with jealousy. I had never been jealous before. I had always considered it a particularly puerile emotion, but I was seething. I wanted to shove you back into your bedroom and force you to change into something else. Some sackcloth, maybe.'

He licked between her breasts, then her nipples. She felt them swell and harden under his moist tongue and she pressed his head down.

When he stopped to take off his clothes, his movements quick and urgent, as though he could hardly bear not to be beside her, she likewise stripped off hers and basked naked under his scrutiny.

'Instead you confronted me in the kitchen and bit my head off,' she said contentedly, and he smiled drily.

'I also, if I recall, tried to get you into bed with me.'

'I wanted to,' Suzanne confessed.

'I know. That was the crazy thing. I knew you wanted me and it was driving me insane, the fact that you just wouldn't give in.'

He stroked her legs and she parted them so that he could feel her desire for him against the palm of his hand.

'Don't you think, as do Angela and Martha, that I was just holding out until the price was right?' She tried to sound light, but her voice was tinged with bitterness and he kissed her lightly at the side of her mouth, while his fingers worked her into a passion that was veering on losing control.

'It never crossed my mind,' he said truthfully. 'You hardly tried to captivate me, did you, with that sharp tongue of yours? Besides, Angela and Martha can only see in people the traits that they see in themselves. Angela wanted me for my money, as Martha wanted my father for his. And got him.'

'And you left because you disliked her.'

'I left because she made a pass at me,' he said flatly. 'My father was still alive at the time, and the woman came into my bedroom one night and tried to persuade me that it would be a good idea to make love. The only reason I stayed on for those last few months was because of Dad. As soon as he died, I couldn't wait to leave the house.'

Suzanne looked at him with horror.

'Is that when you decided to come back and buy the company off her?'

'I decided to do that,' he said, looking at her wryly, 'when I found out how quickly it was going into decline. Dad built that company up single-handedly. Martha was treating it like a board game, dismissing people on personal grounds because they said something she didn't care for. Although, I have to admit that there was an element of vindictiveness in my actions as well.'

'And you very nearly didn't do it.'

'But I did, my darling, I did. Now, no more talk. There are better things to do.' He smiled, his eyes darkening, and they made love with an intensity that left her breathless.

This time there was no holding back, no little voices in her head telling her that she was doing the wrong thing. All those little voices had at last been silenced.

He cupped her breasts in his hands, kissing them, licking them, moving lower so that his mouth trailed along her stomach, down towards that place where all desire began and ended, and she moaned and writhed against his exploring mouth.

She was breathing quickly, eyes closed, when he finally thrust into her with a gentle rhythm at first, then harder and quicker, building up a crescendo of fulfilment.

She felt, at last, as though she had finally found what she had been looking for, she had finally experienced that deep communion of spirit that made everything meaningful.

She turned on her side towards him, stroking his face, enjoying her new-found freedom to express her emotions instead of having to hide them away under wraps in case he caught sight of them.

'Do you know,' he said lazily as she traced the familiar lines of his face with her finger, 'I would have throttled you if you had carried out your hare-brained plan to find somewhere else to live?'

'Would you?' She smiled and felt like the cat that has got the cream.

'No, I would have followed you to whatever hole you had found and made an almighty scene until you were forced to come back with me.'

'How caveman,' she said, laughing.

'Shameful, isn't it?' He guided her hand to him and she circled his throbbing masculinity with her fingers, moving her hand, learning all the time, and liking the uncontrolled desire that made him lie back and yield to the desire she was capable of arousing.

After a while, he put his hand over hers and she knelt over him, leaning forward so that her heavy breasts dangled above him, and he took one nipple into his mouth and sucked hard on it, pulling it into his mouth, and she cried out in pleasure.

When he buried his head between her breasts, she eased her body and slipped onto him, and, like a novice who has discovered the key to everything, she made love to him with the wonder and abandonment of love.

'You wanton thing,' she heard him murmur in a thick voice as she arched back and he took her breasts in his hands, caressing them. And then they were united like a single being, fusing mind and soul, and she closed her eyes the better to enjoy the sweet sensations that filled every minute pore of her body.

It wasn't until darkness began to creep into the bedroom that she realised how long they had lain together.

'I love you,' she told him soberly, and he smiled at her. 'Not that I'm telling you anything that you don't already know.' She was lying on her back, her hair fanning out around her in tangled curls. 'I wanted to die when you told me that I loved you, that you knew I did.'

'And I wanted to shout it out for the whole world to hear. I was so damned smart putting two and two together as far as you were concerned. Not so smart as far as I was concerned.' He paused, and then added, 'By the way, you never said whether you accepted my proposal of marriage or not.'

'After you've been so persuasive? I don't think I could possibly refuse.'

'I'm afraid this will accelerate your moving back up here,' he told her. 'I shall keep the flat on in London, but I want to return here to sort out the company.'

Suzanne didn't answer but she couldn't have been more thrilled by his decision.

She had felt, driving out of the city and away from the constant bustle, that her roots were not in London. London had served its purpose.

'How do you feel about living here? In the house?' he asked her seriously. 'Is it too close for comfort to all your memories of your father?'

'My memories are good ones,' she said. 'It will be perfect living here. Splendid.'

'Feel free to redecorate.' They both laughed at that as thoughts of Martha's extravagant decorations flashed through their heads.

'You might learn to like it if you lived with it for a while,' Suzanne said, grinning.

'But would I ever get accustomed to having to wear sunglasses just so that I didn't get completely dazzled inside some of the rooms?'

'True. That might be a small problem.'

She thought of decorating, of being mistress of this great house which even as the chauffeur's daughter she had loved. What would her father have said if he could have seen them now? He would, she thought, have been happy. He would have been happy with any avenue down which her life took her. She would never alter that cottage in the grounds and when their children grew up they would know the joy of having it there, being able to use it when they wanted.

'How did you feel, seeing Martha leave this place?' he asked, interrupting her thoughts, and she considered the question with a small frown.

'I felt that she had been a very silly woman,' Suzanne told him, sliding her eyes across to his. 'She married for the wrong reasons and then compounded the sin by mismanaging everything after your father died.

'I think, in a way, that she almost couldn't help herself. She found herself in possession of all his wealth and power, with no one to look over her shoulder, and she abused it. Like a petty person who takes pleasure in being a bully with the security of their uniform to protect them. She treated everyone as though they were below her in the pecking order, except those who she considered were of her privileged social standing, and, of course, anyone she thought could do her a favor. I don't think that she ever banked on you returning as an avenging angel.'

'No,' he agreed. 'Three years had made her smug.' He sounded thoroughly satisfied that he had obliterated the smugness from Martha's face, and she felt a lovely warmth seep through her. This was her man now, her lover, husband, friend, protector—all those things and more.

'Aren't you afraid that I might end up like that?' she teased, kissing him lightly on his lips because she just couldn't resist the firm, sexy curve of his mouth, and he smiled with such drowsy, tender warmth that she felt a lump of pure happiness in her throat.

'You? You, my darling, are the pearl in the oyster.' He kissed her back, his tongue lightly lingering on her mouth while his hand moved to cradle her breast. 'I live in fear that someone else is going to discover this fact and do their damnedest to kidnap you.'

'I'm big enough to fight off most potential kidnappers,' she assured him, and he laughed.

'Not to mention outtalk them. Which,' he said, 'brings me to my next proposal.'

She looked at him, puzzled, and he carried on, 'To join the company. You've proved a million times over that you're as bad as me when it comes to digging down to the crux of problems. I want you to run the financial side of the company, at least until it's back on its feet.'

'And then?'

'And then, my love—' he kissed her eyes and held her face in his hands '—who knows? You may not want to work any longer.'

'Really? And what might be the reason for that?'

'You know as well as I do.' He ran his hand along her torso and she sighed with contentment.

'Perhaps I do,' Suzanne conceded. 'Shall we see what we can do about that instead of talking?'

Because nothing could be better than having his child...

Take 2 bestselling love stories FREE

Plus get a FREE surprise gift!

Special Limited-Time Offer

Mail to Harlequin Reader Service®

P.O. Box 609
Fort Erie, Ontario
L2A 5X3

YES! Please send me 2 free Harlequin Presents® novels and my free surprise gift. Then send me 6 brand-new novels every month, which I will receive months before they appear in bookstores. Bill me at the low price of $3.49 each plus 25¢ delivery and GST *. That's the complete price, and a saving of over 10% off the cover prices—quite a bargain! I understand that accepting the books and gift places me under no obligation ever to buy any books. I can always return a shipment and cancel at any time. Even if I never buy another book from Harlequin, the 2 free books and the surprise gift are mine to keep forever.

306 HEN CH7A

Name	(PLEASE PRINT)	
Address		Apt. No.
City	Province	Postal Code

This offer is limited to one order per household and not valid to present Harlequin Presents® subscribers. *Terms and prices are subject to change without notice. Canadian residents will be charged applicable provincial taxes and GST.

CPRES-98   ©1990 Harlequin Enterprises Limited

Coming Next Month

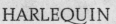